Behind the Walls

MICHAEL LOUIS HEDLEY

Dryad Publishing

First published 2019

Dryad Publishing
www.dryadpublishing.com

ISBN: 978-1-9997857-0-3

DEDICATION

To Hilda with much love.

ACKNOWLEDGEMENTS

To Eamon Carson who was the first to encourage me to write and to my agent Sharon Emery.

1

'Dad! Where are we going?'

I don't know what made me go straight ahead rather than turn our customary right that Saturday, but it has been my pattern of a lifetime not to question such feelings, rather to go along with them and see where they lead. I remember understanding that when I was a boy and talking to friends and family about it and how they used to look at me blankly and not understand what I was saying to them, so much so that I kept quiet, keeping many thoughts to myself and being selective in what I said and to whom I said it.

Going along with those strong messages, that may even come as whispers is important, sometimes the reason becomes abundantly clear very quickly and I recognize it, meeting someone I hadn't seen for ages or spying some item in a shop window I needed to buy and had forgotten about or once crossing a road for no apparent reason other than the strong urge to do so and moments later a car crashed into a wall where I would have been.

Other times I don't know and it doesn't become clear, but the sense that I am being looked after, that I have been protected from something untoward. Angels?

It has been those times that have filled me with a relief that there is more to life than what we perceive as real.

Maybe it was listening to a favourite Tony Bennett CD coming up the road and with a new track starting, 'Stranger In Paradise,' when I was about to turn right prompted me instead to drive straight on.

I was edgy though because I knew our spot, our favoured place for parking, that we'd used since the beginning of the season, that had worked so well for us every match day would be empty, awaiting our arrival, thanks to the intercession of St. Philomena, who always obliged, despite what the Vatican says about her existence. It was a smooth routine, once easily parked, free, safe, then a bite to eat and straight to the ground to enjoy the buzz and excitement of the build-up. So, to try something new was risky, we were later than usual and playing Everton meant there'd be another sell out.

Still, as I say, I always go along with it, but this day it was a strange sensation, going back, back to my childhood and the days I spent as a boy roaming the streets of the city. Here I was up from the Essoldo, Stoll and Pavilion cinemas that were, driving past Sinclair's building, the name still discernible on the brickwork on the side, high up, Sinclair's Tobacco Co., now apartments. Across Westgate Road and up Rutherford Street and onto Blackfriars, by the old city walls. What history! I spotted a stretch of wall, not large, with a gate in it, just a façade with a grassy bank behind rising and dipping to rise again to a car park. That wall. That gate.

I drove on by the brewery, the smells reminiscent of long ago, of the old school, St. Mary's, of the school roof playground in Oystershell Lane, my old school, now demolished, swallowed by the brewery complex. On the roof standing against the railings looking out laughing and joking as the delicious smell of the latest brew wafted across to us.

A space ahead was waiting for us.

'That's lucky finding a spot here so close to the ground, Dad!'

'Hey, mister! Wash your car?'

'Wash my car! It'll fall apart if you wash it, it's only the muck and grime that's holding it together!'

'Dad, he said watch!'

'Oh, yes, of course. How much?'

Mumble.

I fumbled about in the ashtray.

'Here's a pound, that's all the change I have, will that do you?'

'Yeah, mister, that'll do.'

'You'll find us and the car here when you get back.'

The two lads engaged in their enterprise turned away to another potential client.

There was a sudden draught of cold air that touched me deep inside and I froze, caught in a wisp of timelessness. Captured in a moment, my life and times, now, past and future self, roamed in the air to stir memories that rose up from the very essence of existence and purpose of my being. Man and child here now, child and man, then and before, then who knows and future time drawn as well into this space and creation to whirl round in a shadow then again in a light that flashed brightly, held tight, then glimmered, died and was reborn.

Being part, being separate, an outsider looking in, watching from the edge of life and beyond, uncomfortable with a knowledge and an awareness that wasn't understood. As I stood in time and place, now I heard drifting back across the years,

'He lives in a world of his own, a romancer, a dreamer, a little liar.'

Words from my history coming back home to me...

2

'You didn't kiss her at all!'

'Yes I did! I was sitting next to her on the bandstand in the park. We were watching the men putting their instruments away and I turned and gave her a kiss. It wasn't anything very grand, I admit that, just a peck on the cheek, but definitely a kiss for all that!'

'We'll ask her, then we'll see who's a little liar!'

They will as well, I thought, and they're right, I didn't kiss her. We were at the bandstand, we did watch the men packing away their gear, but the rest of it wasn't true. What possessed me to say that I had? I know that I had wanted to, I dreamt that I had, it all seemed so real. They would never understand that. They'd poke and prod me for it. I'd be cast in the role of romancer.

'He gets carried away with himself. He doesn't know the difference between what's real and what isn't. He lives in a world of his own, nothing but a dreamer.'

I knew I had it coming and there was nothing I could do to prevent it. They'd want nothing to do with me. I'd be laughed at, an outcast, for a while. That would pass for sure, but I'd have a few hard days to survive without allies. I could see the vultures gathering for rich pickings. How did I land myself in this predicament? I didn't know at all.

Of course it was the first question they asked Susan at school the next day. Tapper Jones was right there, I bet he hadn't slept all night, he looked so excited, right at the front of the pack, smelling blood. He didn't like me, he thought I'd taken his place on the school football team, so the slightest chance to see me humiliated, he'd be there panting, fangs showing, dripping. And so he was.

'Susan!'

Friendly like, matter of fact, nothing important, by the way, can I have a word with you, only if you have the time, of course.

'Susan!'

Each syllable savoured. Here it comes.

'Susan, did you let him kiss you the other night in the park?'

Silence.

Susan turned from Tapper to me, she was a lovely girl, a pretty face, long golden hair. I was sorry, she had a pained look, then she exploded.

'No I certainly did not! Who has been spreading such a filthy lie?'

'He has!'

The fingers were pointed, there was no escape.

She turned and looked at me, amazed. Tapper was in full swing, the rest silently watched the drama unfolding.

'HE told us that he kissed you when you were at the bandstand the other night.'

'Well that's a load of rubbish, a pack of lies. I wouldn't let him kiss me anyway.'

She turned to me.

'If I hear one word more about it, I'll tell my dad and he'll be up to school and around to your mam's and you'll be for it, so stop spreading lies like that. You hear me?'

I heard, I hung my head in shame. She was furious. I couldn't look at her. I muttered something. I heard her pushing past everybody. I looked up after her as she made to storm off and found some courage to stammer,

'I'm sorry, I don't know what came over me to say that. No, it isn't true at all. I'm sorry.'

She stopped in her tracks as I spoke, but didn't look round, waited until I'd finished then proceeded on her way.

It was the muttering and sniggering of the gathered crowd that burned me. What a fool I felt. The 'Get lost, little liar' didn't hurt as much as the muffled giggles.

Branded as a liar, thrown out, laughed at, not a friend in the world. How did I do it? What should I do?

Well I suppose there was always Matty who'd side with anybody excluded from the main gang because he was always on the outside. He whiffed a bit and was always off the day after the nit nurse came to our school. No, I didn't want to be friends with Matty. If I was going to survive this, I'd do it alone. They'd soon forget, something else would take their attention and I'd return to the fold.

Thankfully I was drenched coming home from school that day and caught a heavy cold. My mam very rarely allowed me to stay off even though I'd insist that I was at death's door, but she could see my miserable state as she tried to rouse me the following morning and decided that I was in the best place and should stay there. And so it was that I was able to enjoy a two-day rest while my mam ferried meals to me at regular intervals and between long bouts of sleep I was able to disappear into a book. I needed this break and I knew it would take the pressure off me at school. By the time I was feeling better it was the weekend, so it turned out to be almost a week after my humiliation before I returned to the fray, school.

I knew there was something different about the class as soon as I walked in. At first I couldn't figure out what it was, but then I realized that there was a new girl. I felt funny when I saw her for the first time. Well, funny is perhaps the wrong word, more weak really, I don't know why. I put it down to my cold as I was still feeling a bit unsteady on my legs. I went over to my usual desk and saw it was filled with a smirking Tapper Jones.

Miss Caws looked up from her desk as she prepared to take the register.

'As you can see we've had a bit of a change round, you'll be sitting there.'

The only empty seat in the room was next to the new girl.

My world had turned upside down. I'd never had to sit beside a girl before, I was the only one. I didn't even get a welcome back from Miss Caws. I'd come to expect that, we didn't like each other. She had her pets and I wasn't one of them, which didn't grieve me at all. The new girl smiled at me as I slumped down in the seat next to her. I smiled back weakly and whispered 'Hi' as Miss Caws started to take the register. I was eager to hear the girls' names being called.

'Margaret Breakwell?'

'Yes Miss.'

Tiny whisper, she always looked sad.

'Dorothy Flynn?'

No reply, that was to be expected, nobody ever saw her in school before 10 o'clock, after *Housewive's Choice* had finished.

'Margaret Johnson?'

'Yes Miss.'

She's getting fat, I'd never noticed that before, she always had more money than anybody else and always had a face full of sweets every break time, so it had eventually taken its toll on her.

'Veronica McGynn?'

'Yes Miss.'

I liked Veronica.

'Irene Martin?'

'Yes Miss.'

It was usually Susan Scott's name, she of recent unhappy memory, that featured next, but it didn't.

'Angela Prentiss?'

The girl next to me replied.

'Yes Miss.'

So it's Angela is it. She didn't sound like the rest of us. I wonder where she has come from. We rarely had any new arrivals at our school, everybody started in Reception and stayed together throughout the school with very few changes. I was eager to find out about her, I couldn't just ask anybody, I could sense that I was still out of favour and if I started chatting away to her, I could imagine what was likely to be the response of the hounds of hell. I'd have to talk to Matty at break.

'Now listen everybody,' Miss Caws poised like a

hungry bird of prey for anybody who dared do otherwise, ready to pounce and devour in one swift vicious swoop. We knew better and were absolutely still and she continued to undivided attention.

'For the next few days you will all have to use the downstairs playground with the little ones, as the roof playground is being resurfaced. For safety's sake there will be no football allowed on the playground, so boys, you will have to restrain yourselves until you're back on the roof.'

What a blow, a severe blow, the world continued to conspire against me, I'd planned to slip gently back into favour through football, I knew I'd still get a game even if nobody was speaking to me. After all, it doesn't matter whether I'm liked or not if I'm scoring a goal or two and I could do that with either foot from most angles. Now with this ban it could make my return to grace more difficult. The bell rang and as Angela left her seat she turned to me and said,

'She doesn't like you, does she?'

She was off before I had a chance to reply. I was impressed.

'Matty, here a minute. Do you want a pineapple chunk?'

'Yeah, thanks. How are you? It's nice to see you back again.'

'Ah thanks Matty, I'm fine now. I see there've been changes since I was last here.'

'You mean the new girl?'

'Well yes, I was thinking that. Do you know much about her?'

'Only what I overheard Mr Kellet say to Miss Caws when he brought her into the classroom for the first time.'

Matty never missed anything. He had the sharpest ears, knew when to slip out unnoticed to sharpen a pencil when two adults were in conversation. He knew he would always be needed if he had something that somebody wanted. Information. He beckoned me closer to him, confiding.

'Apparently her mam and dad have split up, so she's been sent to stay with her granny until everything is sorted out. She's from Nottingham, she talks different from us.'

'I suppose she would, Matty, coming from Nottingham. Do you know where her granny lives?'

'Aye, it's Winchester Street, back off Summerhill Grove beside the park near the bowling green. Miss Caws asked her if she knew her way back there on the first day. She said she did so didn't need anybody to show her.'

Summerhill Grove, that wasn't far from me and I travelled that way regularly when I served Mass at the convent down there. I could well bump into her.

'Thanks Matty.'

'You're welcome.'

I'm sure he wondered why I was so curious. I was beginning to wonder that myself. She seemed different, aware somehow, never noticed that in the class before with anyone. Matty didn't seem to be smelling so much these days and he looked clean. I suppose he must have realized why he was so regularly shunned and had started to do something about it. Maybe he'd finally stopped wetting the bed. If he hadn't realized nobody else would have done, certainly not his dad or his mam who only had time for the drink and beating each other up after they'd both had a skinful. Poor Matty, not much wrong with him, he's not a bad lad.

'Do you want another chunk?'

'Oh, yes please.'

'Go on, help yourself, take a handful.'

I handed him the bag and he took a couple out, putting one in his pocket for later. Come to think of it I'd never seen him with sweets.

Fenced off beside the playground was the air raid shelter from the war. It hadn't been taken down, I suppose the council had more important jobs to do, although the war had been over long enough since, so they'd had the time, maybe they were waiting to see. It was a sinister, squat building, not very inviting. It had been made less inviting by the Head who had threatened to thrash anyone within an inch of his life if he ventured into it.

I noticed Angela playing with a tennis ball by herself, she was bouncing it up and down in a rhythmic manner, a tune running through her I thought. Suddenly the ball squirted off at an angle and arced over the fencing. She looked around briefly then was at the other side in a flash, clearly unseen, but when she picked up her ball, instead of returning to the play area she wandered off towards the entrance of the shelter. I watched her as she moved. It all seemed to be happening in slow motion as I stood transfixed, oblivious of anything and anyone else. Then the bell rang and normal motion seemed to return. I waited awhile, watching the shelter, but Angela did not reappear. Perhaps she was worried she'd be spotted. Maybe she'd decided to run away and this was her chance. Somehow she had managed to get inside and it appeared she was going to stay there. Everyone else obeyed the bell and re-entered the school building, I didn't know what to do. I was torn between two courses of action, should I say anything in case Angela was stuck or in some other danger and needed help, or should I keep quiet? Perhaps she had her reasons for what she had done and didn't want some interfering busybody like me messing things up for her. I was the last one left in the playground.

It came to me in a flash and I knew what I had to do. I ran across the empty yard, scaled the forbidden fence and entered the eerie gloom of the damp shelter, my feet scraping concrete and echoing slightly, waiting for the bombing, the all clear, not seeing anything but darkness until my eyes perceived a little light shafting through the open door A second later I heard a frightened voice.

'My head, my head, it's burning. I can't see very well, please help me, don't leave me.' In the dim light I saw the form of Angela lying there amidst the rubble. I rushed over and took her hand.

'It'll be alright, don't worry, I'll go for help.' She was shivering and didn't want me to go, but I gently slipped my hand out of her clasp. Transfixed for a moment, wanting to stay, yet knowing something very bad must have happened to her, I ran back to the school faster than I'd ever run before.

I burst into the classroom,

'Miss Caws, there's been an accident, it's Angela Prentiss, she's hurt, she's lying in the air raid shelter in a state.'

She knew to believe me. I'd never seen her respond so quickly. She bounded out of the classroom leaving me in charge with a new stick of white chalk, my weapon to use to write down the names of anyone who dared misbehave while she was away. I could hear her scuttling down the corridor to the Head's room. I stood in front of the blackboard surveying my temporary domain, my eyes coming to rest on Tapper Jones. He engaged with me briefly then turned his attention to his work. I was daring him to so much as breathe out of turn and I'd have him, his name would be the first on the board and in the largest letters. He knew it and didn't stir from his tasks. I was disappointed. The rest of the class were busy, but in a more relaxed way. The only sounds were the fading footsteps of Miss Caws and the scraping of ink-charged nibs on exercise books. The near working silence was broken by Mr Kellet and Miss Caws talking excitedly as they rushed along the corridor, past our open classroom door and on down the stairs and out onto the playground. I walked over to the window just in time to see Mr Kellet climb over the fence and make his way into the shelter. I felt a cold wet salamander run down my spine and I shivered. Almost immediately he was out again gesticulating and talking hurriedly to Miss Caws. From my vantage point, it was plain to see that they were both very worried. Miss Caws turned away from Mr Kellet and sprinted across the yard. She'd discarded her shoes, she flew. I'd never realized teachers could run.

Softly she sped along the corridor, she glanced in as she went by. Was there a hint of approval as she noticed the stillness of the room?

Mr Kellet had gone back into the shelter. I watched and waited. The class continued quietly to work. I don't know where my mind had drifted. I must have been lost in my own thoughts because the next thing I remembered was Miss Caws standing next to me, thanking me for looking after the class and sending me back to my place. I glanced at the empty seat next to me and put my hand on it and felt frightened.

We continued to work, but there was a general air of fearful anticipation which grew alarmingly with the sound of approaching bells, followed by screeching brakes, slamming doors, the reassuring echo of strong reliable voices and heavy boots inside the building and without. Miss Caws was standing at the window, holding her hands and rubbing her thumb across her knuckles in a slow methodical manner. She was praying. The class could restrain itself no longer, mathematics became an irrelevance, and as a single silent body we all left our seats to join her at the windows. We were captivated, completely mesmerized by the flurry of activity. I don't think our teacher was fully aware that we were all standing beside her. She crossed herself. I felt heavy. Nobody spoke. Another jangle of fast bells, more footsteps, a stretcher. A tense, waiting emptiness surrounded us. What on earth was happening? I dreaded to think.

After what seemed an eternity, the crumpled body of the blond-haired Angela emerged from the shelter in the arms of a fireman. Mr Kellet was holding her hand and I frowned. Her hair was streaming down behind her head, how long, it swayed slightly as she was carried, her other arm swinging limply. The fireman carefully handed her over to the ambulance men, who laid her out on the stretcher and pulled a blanket up her body to her head. There was a collective intake of breath as we stared. He stopped as it reached her chin and then carefully tucked it in at the sides. She was carried off across and away from our view. Miss Caws crossed herself again, there were tears running down her cheeks. She wiped them away and asked us to join her in a prayer for Angela. Nobody was silly. After we had finished she waved us back to our desks and we all continued to work away to the sound of the accompanying silence. We all felt the same tense atmosphere, we all wanted to know, but nobody wanted to say. We'd encountered the emotions of a drama and didn't understand how to handle them.

Eventually Mr Kellet came in to talk to us, but he couldn't really give us any more information than we'd seen, except that Angela was unconscious when there were those who'd thought that she had gone beyond even that. How damaged she was nobody would know until the doctors had examined her. In the meantime, prayer was all we had for ourselves and for Angela. Mr Kellet summoned me out to the front for a special word of praise, due to my prompt action Angela had a chance; it could well have saved her life.

I didn't know how to respond to that, I kept thinking how rarely I told teachers anything if I could possibly help it and yet this once in my bones, I felt that I should. I always respond to that kind of inner feeling, whatever the consequences. I always have.

The bell rang and it was lunch.

It was stew with fatty meat, small pieces of meat clinging to huge lumps of yellow fat sloshing about in the gravy like grotesque islands of phlegm. I hated fat, the thought of it turned my head, the smell of it turned my nose and the taste of it brought my stomach to volcanic eruption in protest. At our school, nobody was allowed to leave anything at all. Everybody ate everything. There were no exceptions. However, there was a brief slackening of the rule when a mouse was found in the gravy and we were excused from having it, but that was the only time. I surreptitiously put my fat into my handkerchief and kept it in my trouser pocket until the meal was over and I could dash to the toilets and flush the hideous stuff down the pan into the sewers where it belonged. The rest of the meal was miserable, the warm soggy mass gradually seeped through my trouser pocket and reached my leg and started to cool. Nobody had ever discovered my unwanted food disposal system, but my mam often wondered how I managed to get my clothes in such a dirty state, especially my handkerchiefs.

The talk was all about everything except Angela, the noise level rose and rose until it almost reached hysterical proportions, prompting Mr Kellet to ring the hand bell and inform us that if we couldn't talk more quietly we'd have to eat in silence.

In the playground afterwards there was a distinct lethargy about everyone as we moped around, unable to take our eyes off the air raid shelter as if it was some powerful being that demanded our respect.

3

My mam was reading the evening paper when I arrived home. Events at our school had made the front page. It said that a girl had become trapped in an old air raid shelter at her school while playing hide and seek with her friends. When her friends had realized what had happened, they rushed to tell the teacher on duty who summoned help. The girl had been rescued by the fire brigade and an ambulance quickly took her to hospital where she was still unconscious.

'Mam, that's not strictly true. It happened like this.'

I told her the story as it happened without adding anything at all.

'Oh yes,' was all she said, 'don't know what they are doing allowing children to play in there.'

I knew she didn't believe me, she thought I was being fanciful, trying to take centre stage. I just left it rather than argue the toss. It wasn't worth it, but it hurt.

'We aren't allowed to play there,' was all I said.

My mam roused herself from the armchair by the fire and went into the kitchen to make the tea. It was always a fry-up on a Monday of all the leftovers from the Sunday roast. It never failed to be delicious.

'Go and get yourself ready for your tea, otherwise you'll be rushing like a madman.'

Monday night was choir practice at the cathedral. We started at half past six and always finished in enough time to race round for the trolley bus to take us home for the start of *Journey into Space* on the wireless. We couldn't miss that for anything.

I said bye to my mam and left the house as usual with every intention of going to the choir, but suddenly I changed my mind.

'I'm not going tonight, I must find out how Angela is faring. I'll go and see her granny, she'll know.'

With these words running through my head, I found myself outside her house and was debating whether to go ahead and knock. I walked around the bowling green and watched a ladies' pairs game. The competition looked fierce and the players intent on their game. I smiled as I watched, remembering my granny telling me about when I had just learned to toddle and she'd taken me to the park and let me loose. Before she could catch me I was off onto the green, picked up the jack and ran off with it. My granny was embarrassed. The men wanted to be cross because it was a vital end and the home team was winning and it had to be replayed. I went red myself thinking about it now. It happened near the bandstand as well. That memory made me feel even more uncomfortable, so I hurried off to the park leaving the ladies to their bowls and pressed out a drink of water from the old fountain into the chained iron cup hanging at its side. The bitter cold cup and the chilled water woke me into reality. There wasn't anything wrong in wanting to find out how Angela was, I didn't need to be frightened about knocking on the door. I walked quickly back round before I changed my mind again.

It was some time before my knock was answered and I was about to turn and walk away when I heard the shifting of bolts, the clinking of chain and the turning of the lock. The door opened. A small, hunched, white haired old lady with a blanket wrapped round her bowed shoulders stood before me. She had a lovely smile and bright eyes.

'I've come to see about Angela,' I blurted out without even saying hello.

'I wondered if she was alright. I'm from the school, I sit next to her. It was me who told the teacher about her being in the shelter. I feel responsible somehow. How is she?'

This all rushed out in a flood and was almost too much for the old lady, who stood looking at me, bewildered. There was a pause, then,

'Ee, lad, well now, you'd better come in and we'll have a talk about it.'

I was taken through into the kitchen, warm and cosy, the soft coal firelight dancing on the flowered wallpaper, the kettle singing to itself on the hob of the black leaded stove.

'Would you like a cup of tea, son? I was just about to have one myself.'

She was very like my granny who'd offer a cup of tea to anyone who called. It was the way. I accepted the invitation and before long I was sipping tea from the best china while I sat in a snug old leather armchair by the fire. I felt spoilt. Out came the biscuits. The old lady was fussing about and didn't seem able to settle. She stood before me apologetically wringing her arthritic hands.

'I'm sorry, I've not had the chance to visit the hospital, you know. It's my legs, they're not as good as they used to be. I don't cross the doors much these days. The kind headmaster's been up to see Angela and she's going to be alright. She's had a nasty bump, but she's conscious now. They're going to keep her in for observation and do some tests, to be sure.'

She looked a sad soul standing before me, old and frail, unable to cope with this sudden intrusion into the gentle pattern of her life.

'Would you like me to go up with you on the bus?'

She suddenly became less agitated and still.

'I'd like to go and see for myself, but I'm not up to it. Will you go for me?'

I was quite taken aback by her direct request.

'I don't know if they'd let me in, not being a relative, they're very strict up at the General.'

'Oh, I'm sure they would.' As I hadn't rejected her request outright, she warmed to her task of convincing me that I'd be welcomed on her behalf.

'If I give you a letter to take from me to Angela, you could deliver it, I'll give you a few apples and biscuits as well. I'm sure the ward sister won't mind.'

I wanted to go. I didn't want to appear too eager but this was the time.

'Well, if you'd really like me to, I will.'

'Oh, good, that's grand. You know the way?'

I nodded, feeling the back of my head as I did so, the scar remained where four stitches had been inserted and removed there.

The old lady shuffled off to write her letter as I sat and watched the fire. Before long I was saying goodbye and was off with letter in one hand and a bag of biscuits and apples in the other.

I took the bus up to the hospital. There was a steady stream of people walking in, so I'd arrived at the proper visiting time.

The sister wouldn't let me in at first, but when she saw the letter, the biscuits and the fruit and my pleading face, she agreed.

'Hello Angela.'

She looked at me blankly at first, I didn't suppose she would recognize me; we had hardly communicated much in class and the shelter was traumatic. The ill effects, her head all bandaged. I explained to her quickly how I happened to be there, before she had the opportunity to say I don't know you, but the light clicked on as I started speaking and she said,

'She doesn't like you much!' She smiled and shuffled across the bed to be closer to where I stood. I pulled up a chair, gave her the letter and arranged the gifts from her granny on the bedside cabinet and stuffed the bag in my trouser pocket.

A distant clock chimed the half hour, the theme tune of *Journey into Space* would be breaking over the airwaves, I'd never missed an episode before tonight, even though I was worried about Captain Jet Morgan and the crew after they had encountered a fleet of UFOs at the end of last week's episode, yet tonight I was unconcerned.

'I'm glad you ran for help.'

I nodded and understood why she said that.

'I'm sure Miss Caws will think better of you for all you did.'

I shrugged and dismissed it, what she thought would never affect me.

I looked at her with her appealing stark white bandage fastened around her head, giving her hair and face a Nordic Indian look. She still looked pale.

'How are you feeling now?'

'I don't know really, I feel weak and my memory of it is a bit vague, but I remember you coming in and was pleased that I wasn't on my own anymore. I think I'll be alright. The doctors seem to be reassured, I'm sure they'll let me go back to my granny's if everything goes smoothly. They've a few more tests to do, but after that I'll just need to rest.'

'So, do you have any idea when they will allow you to go home?'

'Tomorrow maybe.'

'As soon as that! I think you will be lucky.'

'We'll see. Will you come and see me when I do?'

This was new to me.

'If you'd like me to, I will, eh, yes of course.'

'Good, I'd like that. Thank you for bringing the letter and those. Say thanks to my gran and tell her not to worry about me.'

It was then that the ward sister approached.

'You've had more than ten minutes, young man!'

And she swept me away.

I rushed out down Westgate Road. I'd wanted to go home, but felt that I should go and reassure her granny. I ran all the way to her house, delivered the message and made for home. I slowed my speed as I approached our gate. *Journey into Space* had long since finished by the time I opened the front door.

'Where the hell have you been?' I've been worried sick!' was my mam's hello. I told the truth and was belted for it.

'You're too young to be bothering with lasses, you'll

end up the same as your father.'

He'd gone and left us for another woman a couple of years earlier. I was regularly told at times like these that I had his badness; this was yet another example of it seeping out. I didn't understand. I went to bed and wished that I was free.

The moon filtered through the curtains. There was a slight breeze. I watched dancing shadows on the wall, calling me with their movements the swaying, to and fro of water onto a beach, I saw dancers on the sand gliding softly to the motion of the waters, I tasted the salt of my tears as I fell asleep crying silently, alone.

4

I woke early, Tuesday, I was serving Mass at the convent and I had to be there for five to seven. How clear the morning was. The shift workers out in their refreshingly reassuring overalls, khaki bait bags, a relic from army days, slung over their shoulders, hair heavily Brylcreemed, were on the move, the *Daily Mirror* in evidence under their arms, the first cigarette between their lips. Road sweepers were freshening up the streets, the clink clank of milk bottles. The trolley buses pulled away sleepily in opposite directions, Milligan's Bakery smelt alive.

Silently, the doorkeeper at the convent allowed me access. Silence and meditation were the order of the early morning. I'd offer up my Mass for Angela's recovery. The sister sacristan spoke to me.

'We at the convent have heard from the wireless that a bishop has run off with his housekeeper, a dreadful wicked lie to be sure, but could you possibly bring us any newspaper clippings of the story the next time you come to serve?'

'Yes Sister, of course, I'll do my best.'

They weren't allowed any newspapers, but they did like to keep in touch at the convent. My aunt Vera always bought the *News of the World*, they'd be sure to run the story. Sister Mary Vincent would enjoy their version.

The priest came into the sacristy and I went to light the candles on the altar. By the time I returned, Father Keen was ready to be led to the altar. I don't think he enjoyed saying Mass at the convent as he always tore through it at breakneck speed. That suited me as I was starving. Missing out on my supper had started to take its toll, my stomach was rumbling. Mass proceeded at the pace of a Charlie Chaplin film, but somehow still managed to maintain its dignity. I left the convent after extinguishing the candles and folding away the vestments. There was an inch of wine left in the cruet. As there was little point in putting it back in the bottle and it was a chill morning, I knocked it back. The warm glow was pleasing and helped me home with an extra spring in my step.

My mam wasn't talking to me at breakfast. I suspected that she was still upset about last night, but it could have been anything, it happened often since my dad left. We might as well have been in the convent. I was glad to go to school.

It was just before lunch when Mr Kellet came in to tell us that Angela's doctors were pleased with her and were sending her home.

She was all right.

'She'll be going home today, but she'll have to rest up for a few days, until she's completely well.'

You could hear the relief in his voice. We had plenty to watch at break time as in the distance the council men with their windy hammers were finally starting to knock down the old shelter. The extra space would make a big difference to the playground.

Mr Sampson had asked to see a number of boys after we'd eaten lunch: mince pies, no trauma. He had arranged a football match against St. Vincent's Orphanage after school. I was playing, Tapper was reserve.

I'd never been to an orphanage before and I was a little apprehensive. My mam used to regularly threaten to put me in one if I kept on behaving like my dad. She said she'd have no more to do with me, she even had her hat and coat on one day and had me out of the house until I bawled and pleaded for another chance. After last night and the continued bitterness this morning, I thought that the last place I wanted to play football was at an orphanage. Perhaps my mam and Mr Sampson had deliberately arranged it all to get me up there on false pretences and once through the door the lock would turn behind me and that would be me, lost. I shuddered at the thought and was more than a little apprehensive as we arrived at the gates of St. Vincent's later in the afternoon.

I was surprised at the pleasant atmosphere. Everybody was so friendly that my fears quickly evaporated and I was happy to pull on my yellow and blue shirt and trot out onto the pitch. The grass was a bit long, on a slight slope, but it would do fine. I loved being out with a ball at my feet.

The reality of the game hit me soon enough as the goals piled up against us. These lads knew their own patch well and before long we were four goals down and on the verge of complete humiliation. It was only a friendly, but they kept sending on fresh men every few minutes when the others got tired, which didn't seem fair. Our teacher was the referee and he didn't seem to mind at all. That annoyed me.

It was half time and we sloped off, demoralized, some wanting to go home. Mr Sampson didn't say anything, he let us suck on pieces of orange while he chatted to their lads. It was me who spoke as he blew the whistle for the restart.

'Come on lads, enough of this. Let's show them what we're made of!'

We needed something to stir us as we started the second half. I'd somehow acquired something after yesterday and they responded to my exhortation. Jimmy Leach pulled one back almost straight from the kick-off. It went in off the backside of a defender, but we needed some luck. Our spirits rose, a glimpse of light appeared and our pace quickened. All might not be lost. Armstrong headed in from a corner, his ginger head meeting the ball squarely, it flying just out of their goalie's reach. Two back. A few minutes later, we'd never played as well, Kelly was pulled down in the box. A clear penalty. I didn't feel any nerves as I blasted it home. Three. 4-3, a much more respectable score-line altogether, honour nearly restored. With very little time left, Armstrong pushed the ball through the middle over the half-way line and I galloped after it. I could see Mr Sampson looking at his watch and getting his whistle ready to blow for full time, I was sure he didn't want us to draw, never mind win, I knew that if I ran through the defence I wouldn't have time to complete the scoring. I was sure he'd blow the whistle just as I was about to round the goalkeeper and slot the ball gently into an empty net. He'd seen me do that often enough before and that's what he was waiting for. I sensed that the rest of the lads were thinking the same. I let fly from forty yards and it hit the back of the net before Sampson had a chance to blow for full time. I could see him looking around for a possible reason to disallow it, but in the end he pointed back to the centre spot for the restart. Four all. What a fight back. He blew for the end a moment later. We were delighted with ourselves and couldn't talk about anything else as we changed and had orange juice and biscuits, reliving every glorious moment of our resurrection from the dead. I was back as well. Tapper didn't look pleased.

On the way home we reckoned that Sampson wanted the orphanage team to win because he felt sorry for their plight. I felt the same, I thought I was going to be one of them, but I didn't think they'd appreciate that kind of sympathy, I wouldn't. I must say I was glad when I was out of the gates and on my way home.

Nobody was interested in the match when I arrived home except my mam complaining about having to do more washing as if she didn't have enough to do. There didn't seem to be much pleasure in her life since my dad left. I think she missed him, saw him in me and took it out on me. She should find herself someone else instead of losing herself in housework and making me miserable. Life was such a chore for her and I didn't know what I could do to help. She saw me looking at her and her eyes changed, she'd been beautiful once, before the break-up, soft, not hard like now. Suddenly she relented a little.

'Here's a shilling, bonny lad, go and fetch us a couple of ice creams.'

She touched me on the arm when she gave me the

money. She still was beautiful, I could feel her warmth, her sadness flooding into me.

'Go on now, son, before it gets too dark,' then she bustled off back into the kitchen. The floor needed washing.

We sat by the firelight and ate through the chocolate, the vanilla and finally the strawberry layer in a gentle bubble of peace before it burst again and she was back in the kitchen and I was off to bed.

A mention was made of our football match at assembly and how well we played and were a credit to the school. It was a pleasant feeling, standing up before the rest of the school and accepting the applause. I wished that Angela had been there, I wondered about her off and on throughout the day, eager to know if she'd actually come home. I decided to go and find out for myself after school. I wanted the day to pass quickly so I could be off and away, but it didn't, quite the opposite. Everything seemed to slow down and the time dragged out the course of the day. The bell called its final tune and I was about to rush out when I was called back. Mr Sampson wanted to see me. What now? It had to be trivial.

'Don't forget to bring your football strip back clean by the weekend.'

Angela's granny answered the door.

'Hello Mrs Prentiss, is she back from the hospital?'

The old lady's face lit up and she waved me in.

There was Angela sitting all huddled up by the fire, still pale, but her smile said what words didn't.

I was content to be there. We talked a lot. I was eager to tell her all about the football and the dramatic ending to the game and she told me how the tests had gone and how relieved she was to be out of hospital. I couldn't remember ever being so voluble. Colour seemed to come back to her face as we chatted, it may have been the fire. Her granny seemed pleased and lighter on her feet when she came in with a drink for me and announced that she was going out on a few errands. She seemed happy to leave us on our own. I volunteered to go for her, but no, a trip to the shops was something she felt she could manage, she enjoyed going when she could and it prevented her joints from seizing up altogether and besides, she needed to catch up with all the gossip. She laughed as she left the room.

We continued to talk, the flow of conversation was free and endless, there seemed so much to say. I asked her about her mam and dad.

They'd always been fighting, as long as she could recall, shouting at each other, living their own separate lives, staying together just for her sake. She'd heard them say that.

'If it wasn't for Angela I'd walk out now and never come back.'

'And so would I!' replied her dad as Angela had walked in on one of their rows and started yelling and shouting at both of them to stop it and that she didn't want to be there with them on those terms. She didn't wish to live her life like that. They hadn't answered her or tried to comfort her and didn't try to make it up. It was past that stage. She started staying away from school, spending her time walking around the city and its parks when the weather was fine and mooching around the shops when it was wet. She'd dreamed her dreams around the fancy window displays, seeing herself in the newly fashioned kitchens and bedrooms and plush carpets with the lushest of piles to sink into in elegant living rooms. Her abiding dream was one of luxury and warmth in a happy home. She started staying out late at nights, not wishing to go home. She would go into the cinema and watch the same movies over and over till the Queen came on and everyone rushed out home.

Nobody seemed concerned when she didn't arrive home, she had to make her own food anyway and often she was the only one at home.

'I couldn't understand how they could both say that they were staying together for me, when neither of them bothered.'

I was sad to hear her talk, I recognized some of it. Then her mam took off, without a note, no explanation, no goodbye.

'She went in the clothes she'd gone off in to work in the morning. I remember seeing her standing at the kitchen door while I was eating my toast. All she said was, "Well, I'll be off." And away she went. She didn't take anything with her. She wanted a complete break from it without any memories. I cried a lot when I realized that. I felt unwanted, unloved and alone.'

I could feel choking in my throat as she spoke and I had to turn away from her for a moment.

'Come on, let's have a piece of toast, that fire there is perfect for it. I'm sure your gran won't mind. Don't you move!'

Suddenly I felt light and happy as I rummaged around and found a toasting fork and a couple of crusts perfect for the job.

I knelt by the fire, whistling unconsciously.

'What's that tune? I recognise it.'

'That's a surprise, my whistling's awful.'

I sang and she joined in to 'Stranger In Paradise.'

Together we said, 'Tony Bennett!'

I smiled, 'My mam loves him.'

Angela nodded, choked, 'So does mine.' Her head dropped.

The smell of the toast wafted around the room. What a joy.

'Just look at that, a golden brown.' I lashed on the butter for it to melt immediately, dripping over the sides and onto the plate.

'Nothing better to make you comfortable.' We sat there in silence enjoying every mouthful, with the occasional 'Mm,' and the smacking of lips. The sinking spell had been broken and we were flying high. She continued her story unbidden. Her father had written to his mam and that's how she came to be here until everything was sorted out. Whatever that really meant she didn't know. Hence her sudden appearance out of the blue. I listened transfixed by her talking. I was discovering a gentleness in her and a level of communication deeper than I'd ever experienced with anyone. The words seemed to mean more. They had a richness that was new to me.

'I wonder what it would be like to live at peace with someone and be really happy?'

'I don't know. I can't say that I've ever experienced it. That's something I've dreamed about often, when I used to hear my mam and dad arguing and I lay awake late into the night and tried to find somewhere to hide from it all.'

'I understand that. Wouldn't it be great if we could find somewhere for ourselves to go, a little place of our own, happy and peaceful.'

'Nice to dream.'

She turned and looked at me with an engaging

strength.

'If we could find that place, I'd be so happy.'

Angela's granny returned then and started fussing about the kitchen. I took this as my signal to leave. I promised to return the following day.

'What's up Mam?' She was standing ironing in the kitchen, tears streaming down her cheeks.

'It's not the same, I haven't got over the other week, probably never will.'

She held up her iron pointing it towards the wireless hanging on the wall.

I realised then that she must have been listening to her favourite programme. The Archers.

Grace Archer had died trying to rescue her horse Midnight from the fire that had broken out in the stables. A beam had crashed down on her as she tried to push her way into the blaze. My Mam had cried buckets the day when it happened and she was clearly still distraught. It was a monumental tragedy. The Archers would never be the same again. There was Phil Archer without a wife, my Mam and me without my Dad and now Angela with nobody, ticking over with her Granny. Life.

'Never mind Mam. I'm sure it'll pass soon enough.'

She shook her head and wiped her eyes on her pinny and gestured me to the kitchen door.

It didn't seem fair.

I lay in bed wondering what I could possibly do about it all.

I began imagining the places Angela and I could go together, how she and I would be gentle with each in our own little place. I fell asleep thinking of just that.

I woke with a start, sweating, shaking and

frightened, I dreamed that I had been with Angela caught up in a fire in a locked barn without means of escape. The flames grew higher as we stood holding onto each other, unable to move from where we stood as we grew hotter and hotter, with the tongues of the fire furiously whipping around us and determined to devour us.

I was shivering with the cooling sweat, my throat was parched. I was desperate for a drink. I needed to break the dream spell by getting out of bed and moving around. I was very quiet on my feet as I went into the bathroom. I changed my pyjamas, drying the sweat off me as I did so. The cold drink bit into my parched throat, the sensation taking away the nearness of the dream, the water seemed to seek out the hidden fires in me and dowse them.

At ease, I tiptoed back to my room, I heard sobbing coming from across the way. I stopped outside the room wondering what to do. Realizing that there wasn't anything that I could do, reluctantly I slipped past and into my own room quietly closing the door and sliding back into bed, pulling the covers over my head.

Despite that I didn't sleep much afterwards, more in snatches as I tossed and turned, seeing faces in my head, crying faces coming up large then fading fast into the distance. Angela, my mam, my dad, me, faces in tears flowing red, all the eyes were sad, inward looking, searching for peace. I couldn't shake those images, they plagued me till I heard the milkman at the front door and I knew my ordeal was over and I could get up.

5

'Get your own breakfast son, I'm not up to it this morning, I'll just stop in bed. Don't bring me anything up.'

'Alright Mam. I'll see you tonight.'

Miss Caws informed us after taking the register that there was a special treat in store for us in the afternoon. We were going out as a class to look at part of the old west walls, to make some sketches of them. It was unusual to go anywhere from school, so it was indeed something special. As we were to be on our best behaviour, Miss Caws paired us off in a boy girl arrangement to ensure the maintenance of near perfect order. Veronica McGynn was my partner which suited me fine as I liked talking to her. She was good at art as well, so she'd help me with my drawings because I was hopeless. I could never make the connection eye to mind to pencil to paper. I couldn't fathom the organization of that at all. I seemed to have some sort of mental blockage there. I was better making a word picture, I enjoyed doing that, I could see pictures very clearly that way.

After lunch, armed with clipboards, paper, pencils and rubbers, we lined up in our pairs outside the school. The workmen were hard at the demolition of the remnant of war in our community. The yard looked strangely incomplete without it, like a wasteland where nothing could ever grow.

We marched off down Oystershell Lane towards the old city walls. It didn't take us long to reach our goal and to be sitting on the grass listening to Miss Caws bring to life the old city protected by these walls. I'd never before realized how small the city had been, I'd always imagined it large. How sensible of the people to live inside the walls for safety and protection. It was amazing when Miss Caws asked,

'How many of you have noticed the walls before today?'

Very few hands were raised in reply, mine wasn't one of them, even though I'd walked past them on numerous occasions. I'd always thought they were part of a walled garden or the remains of some old building long since broken down and forgotten.

'Now I don't need to say anything about behaviour, do I?'

The question defied answer.

'You may go anywhere up this stretch of wall and sketch where and what you wish, as long as you keep in sight of me.'

Veronica and I walked up away from the rest and sat down.

'Will you do a rough outline for me, please?'

'Of course.'

'Thanks.'

No fuss. I liked that. While she was doing it, I walked up to the wall to feel it. I closed my eyes, looking for pictures of it being built, of the men working away at it, of its life. Although it was rough, it had a warm, friendly feel, secure even after all this passage of time. The townsfolk would have rested easy at nights knowing that they were well protected. As I followed the wall around, I spotted a small postern door. The doorway was old, not so the door. I looked through a crack to see what lay behind, suddenly I felt a great surge of excitement build up inside me, my heart was thumping away, my eyes captured the scene totally, instantly and beyond it. A walled garden with a hut at the far end of it. The hut looked small and solid. I heard Veronica calling me. Further exploration would have to wait for a more suitable opportunity. I was convinced that I'd been directed to that place, that hut. It wasn't a coincidence.

It was for Angela and me. That's where we could go. I could see it all clearly.

'Where've you been?'

'I was looking behind the walls that's all. I didn't realise I'd been gone that long.'

'Well you have, I was getting worried, I thought Miss Caws was going to come and find you gone. I don't know what I would have told her. You'd have been for it. You know what she's like.'

'Well nothing happened, did it? You needn't have worried. Why did you want to worry about me anyway?'

Nobody at school had ever expressed concern about me before, most people rather liked the idea of others being in trouble. They enjoyed the spectacle of a ranting, raving teacher and a quaking, unnaturally subdued child, thinking to themselves, 'Thank God it's not me, but this is fun.'

'I don't know, it's difficult to explain. Oh, if you must know I don't like to see you in trouble, it makes me feel sad. Now here, I've finished your sketch, I'll need to start on my own!'

I looked at what she had done for me, it was very good, she'd taken a lot of care over it. I went over it with a thicker pencil, adding bits of my own that largely detracted from her workmanship, but it looked more like my own work, but really a lot better than I could have done.

'Are you happy, Veronica?'

'Whatever do you mean by that?'

'Are you happy? That's all. Do you enjoy yourself? Are you happy at home? Do you like the things you do?'

'I don't know, those are not things that I have thought about at all. I suppose I'm happy. I look forward to going home after school. I know that I'm not unhappy. Is that the same thing?'

'I'm not sure but go on, keep talking.'

'I enjoy most things I do. I fight with my brother a lot at home. He's rotten to me, but it's never very serious and I soon forget about it. You are funny asking those questions. Why did you ask?'

'I can't say really. I've been thinking about being happy recently that's all. I wondered whether people took time to think about it much or accepted what they had as being normal.'

'I think it's considered normal to be happy, most people have it and don't give it much thought because it's what they expect.'

I nodded, most people have it, because it's what they expect. I wonder, is it as simple as that? If it is, how lucky most people are.

'I'm glad for you Veronica, it suits you to be happy and it makes you kind.'

I received an 'Uh huh, yes that's fine,' comment for my sketch. Miss Caws drooled over Veronica's, it was so good.

'That will look lovely on display.' No doubt implying that mine would be best suited for the classroom waste bin. By the time we arrived back at school it was time for prayers and home.

6

I had other plans before going home. I retraced my steps and there I was in front of the doorway once again. Now I had plenty of time to explore. There wasn't a soul about, so I climbed the door and let myself gently down the other side into the garden. How strange this walled garden with its shed; it didn't seem to belong, the shed, the walls, the garden, me in it and yet they all welded into something that was right. I walked over to the shed.

The door wasn't locked so I went in. It was dark, the windows thick with dust. There was a splay legged iron stove at the far end with its chimney stretching up through the roof. There was a workbench with three stools by it. The floor was wooden and bare apart from tufts of weeds that had forced their way up into the unknown. I opened a cupboard and found some rolled papers on a shelf. I took them over to the door. They were plans of the old city with its walls intact. Miss Caws would relish a look at these. I dismissed the notion as quickly as I had entertained it. The maps were heavily marked with notes and comments. I made out one scribble, 'Possible site for exploratory excavation.' These probably belonged to the archaeology department at the university or the council or both. There was always news of something cropping up from ancient times that warranted investigation. Another note about where I stood, 'Friary garden?' I could picture the friars bustling around, picking vegetables, sampling the juicy plump strawberries. A figure came into my head. He smiled at me before pulling his hood up. I shivered.

I put the papers back in the cupboard and stood by the stove. What had been gnawing at me suddenly blossomed with a shaft of sunlight bursting through the door and lighting up the shed. This would be our home. For Angela and me. It was perfect. Clean windows. A carpet. The stove blazing. The door shut behind us and we'd have a place of warmth and peace to share. Happy? I closed the door carefully behind me and walked back over the grass to the walls. There was a cold water tap on its own, the grass had been cut, its last before the spring. Everything was still. I touched the walls, closed my eyes and slowly walked around, picturing flowers growing beside a bright red summer house in the corner with a blonde-haired girl in a white dress skipping round, laughing. Behind her a friar in a black and white habit was kneeling, his head bowed.

I climbed back over the wall, carefully checking, as I peeped over the top, that nobody was watching. I hauled myself over and down, falling as I dropped. I picked myself up. The street was deserted. I looked back at the door. The lock could easily be unscrewed for access when necessary. I didn't want Angela climbing over that wall even though she'd be capable of it. Anyway, I might have a key to fit it. I collected keys, I had hundreds of them. I didn't like coming across locked doors or cupboards. I needed to know what lay behind, that's what started me collecting in the first place. My mam kept a number of doors and cupboards locked without offering me any adequate reason when I asked. One cupboard I managed to open was filled with dry foodstuffs and boxes of sugar cubes. There must have been years of supplies, a throwback to the war with all its shortages and the prospect of it all happening again. Ration books were well remembered. My real find of treasures was in my mam's bedroom sideboard.

I'd been saving that room for the right occasion. My mam was going to take a pie she'd made around to her eldest sister who'd not been well. I knew she would be gone a decent time, so I took the opportunity for a good long rummage. I hunted through my box of keys till I found one that fitted and clicked open. There were all sorts inside. I found a bag filled with sovereigns and crowns dating back years. There were some trophies as well, one with a footballer standing on the lid with a ball in his hand, some with racing greyhounds and one with a couple dancing. I was fingering my way further back into the cupboard when I heard the sound of returning footsteps, so I had to move fast. By the time my mam saw me I was coming down the stairs by way of my bedroom to put away my keys.

'Hello Mam, you've been quick.'

She gave me one of her looks. She didn't say anything, but she knew that I'd been up to something. I'd always been extra careful after that close shave. That's why I checked instinctively that the coast was clear before dropping over the wall, it had become part of my built-in defence system.

I thought as I'd be late home, I'd better take the trolley bus to save any unwanted questions.

The nuns had Benediction on a Thursday evening and I had to serve, so I could slip round to Angela's after I finished at the convent.

That felt like a good idea. I'd be able to tell her about the hut, the garden and my vision for it. I was excited at the prospect. I nipped over to my aunt Vera's and cut out the pieces about the bishop and his housekeeper before making my way to the convent. My mam didn't seem to worry too much about the time I arrived home from there, I could hardly be up to any mischief. It was a regular occurrence for the priest to be late or for the nuns to suddenly decide to add a few extra hymns or fit in a couple of decades of the rosary, so I'd be able to slip around to Angela's afterwards without attracting any undue suspicion. The doorkeeper always had a smile for me on Benediction nights.

'God evening, Sister Agnes.'

Smile, nod, no words. I wonder what she thinks about all the time, not speaking. Sister Mary Bernard was hovering in the sacristy, like a debt collector ready to be paid in full, rubbing her hands, her beads chinking at her side.

'Hello Sister, I have those cuttings you asked for from last Sunday's papers, they have the whole story. I'll keep my eye open for any follow up.'

'Thank you, my son', were her few words to me as she scuttled off, thrusting the damning evidence, her treasures, deep into the long black pocket of her habit, leaving only the breeze as evidence of her presence. My mam reckoned that Sister Mary Bernard wasn't that well, filling up with water, needed regular treatment. I didn't understand the condition, but I was always conscious of looking closely at her to see if I could detect any changes in her appearance. I often thought her face looked bloated, but I put that down to her wimple being too tight, I'd also heard that she had a very healthy appetite.

There was always spiritual reading left for me while I waited for the priest to arrive. Six o'clock Saints for me to-night. I read the story of St. Jerome and the lion whose paw he had tended and who worked for him guarding the donkey and woodcutter from rogues and robbers. It was an enthralling tale. I drifted off, picturing Angela and I in our hut with a lion prowling the gardens and protecting us at the same time. The priest bursting in stirred me to instant action. I went to light the candles, the priest acknowledged my existence with a nod. The incense was burning well in the thurible and I savoured the aroma, I sprinkled some more over the glowing pieces of charcoal to make a rich thick smog, then processed with the priest onto the altar, swinging the thurible in vigorous, flamboyant manner as I led the way.

'*O Salutaris hostia,*' started the nuns, O Saving Host. I prayed for happiness, thought about Angela in our little hut.

By the time I had snuffed out the candles the priest had gone. I took off my cotta and cassock, hung them in the cupboard and left. Nobody said thank you or goodbye. I was just taken for granted, performing a useful function, but nothing more. I didn't want praise, but an awareness, an acknowledgement that I was alive and counted for something. It was as if I didn't exist for these people, I didn't affect their lives in any way so I wasn't considered until I could be used to smuggle in dubious newspaper cuttings. Saddened by the thought, I slammed the convent door behind me, back heeled it to with gusto to check it was shut properly, then walked round to Angela's house.

The tea tasted pleasant, Angela's granny was listening to the wireless, Angela looked much improved. She had made the tea for us, I took the milk and sugar out of the kitchen safe.

'How do you feel to-day?'

'Fine, really, there isn't anything wrong with me now, apart from an occasional twinge in my head. I'm fully recovered, I could go back to school tomorrow, but Granny says I have to see the doctor first, so it'll probably be Monday before I return. If I go to the doctor's in the morning there would be little point in coming back in just for an afternoon.'

I couldn't wait any longer.

'I've found a little place, I think you'd like it. It's only small, but size doesn't affect happiness. It's not far from here, would you like to see it?'

'See it! You know I would, it sounds exciting. When can I come?'

'I thought if you're well enough, I'd meet you after school tomorrow outside the Essoldo. Do you know where that is?'

'Yes I've seen it, it's down the hill. I'll be well enough.'

'Agreed then, I'll meet you, we'll go and have a look together and you can tell me what you think.'

'Tell me some more about it, please. Please!'

I was tempted to do so, she appeared so desperate

to know, but I was firm.

'No, I'm not, I'll spoil it, I won't describe it properly and you'll build up a false picture. I can't. Please be patient and let it grow naturally, enjoy dreaming about it. Get a feel for it.'

'I think you're rotten, but I suppose you're right. I'll enjoy preparing myself for it.'

'Now listen, you must promise me that if the doctor doesn't pass you fit, healthy and fully recovered, you won't come. Promise. We don't want to take any risks with you.'

She was touched by my concern, I could tell by the way she looked at me. She promised and then smiled. And so it was agreed.

I took my leave of them both, her granny was asleep by the wireless. I didn't disturb her, tiptoeing by then out into the cold night and hurried home in the dark.

My mam was sitting beside the fire darning a pair of my school socks when I made my gentle entrance.

'Hello Mam.'

'Hello son. It's time for your bed.'

'Alright Mam. Goodnight.'

'Goodnight son.'

Our talking rarely seemed to progress much further than that. She was always preoccupied with her own weary thoughts, her own private misery. I made myself a toasted crust and marmalade in front of the fire, had a glass of milk, put on another shovelful of coal and went to bed. After my mam had said goodnight, I don't think she noticed all my activity, she continued to sit, methodically darn and let the fire warm her. I could well have not been there.

Dreams come quickly in the night, staying with me till waking. I saw visions of green, and blue with reds turning to softness, then becoming bright sunshine yellow, blistering with goodness and awe. There were voices hiding in the shades of lightness, calling me on, the sensations changed their shaping, appearing as people I'd never seen before, but they knew me. They were smiling. Then in the misty haze I saw a face I did recognize. It was the friar in the black and white habit and he was waving to me. Houses, gardens, seas all joining together in flames, burning brightly, then fading to leave a silent blackness with a dim spot of pale light in the distance. I didn't wake up frightened. I woke up and remembered, my arm out from the covers waving back.

7

Boiled eggs on Friday, never any meat, fish and chips for lunch, tripe and onions for tea, but never for me, I was spared that horror. Instead I had mashed potatoes with melted butter, beans and a fried egg. I don't know how anybody could eat tripe.

The highlight of the school day was a visit from the old Canon who on occasion came in to check up on our religious knowledge. Miss Caws stood behind him, white with worry, and acting as if somehow trying to wash her hands of us. She leaned heavily against her desk as she listened to some of the pathetic answers some of us gave despite the fact that she was attempting to mouth saner responses for us to pick up. It was a regular torture for her.

Today after all the usual questions the Canon suddenly wondered whether anybody knew whose feast day it happened to be.

Miss Caws stopped moving her hands, her mouth hung open, without shaping an answer.

She didn't know.

You could have heard a pin drop, he had a way of looking at us that penetrated our souls.

We didn't like it, Miss Caws slumped even further behind him, waiting.

His face said it all when there wasn't a single hand raised. He turned, about to voice a sharp comment to a distraught Miss Caws when I coughed loud, but apologetically and slowly edged up my hand.

Miss Caws looked up worried, concerned, hopeful,

'St Jerome, Canon?'

A beam changed the Canon's normally severe face.

'Well done lad, how did you come to know that?'

I cleared my throat and stood up, a solitary figure in my desk with Angela of course still absent from the seat beside me. I felt alone.

Then suddenly as I breathed in, I felt confident because I really knew.

'I remember reading a story about him and it stayed with me. He tamed a lion by removing a thorn out of its front paw. The poor animal had been in terrible pain. I think he's the patron saint of schoolchildren, but the book didn't say why. It said the thirtieth of September is his feast day and that's today.'

The Canon continued to show approval.

'Well done, well done lad, well done. He became famous for a lot of things as well, which I'm sure Miss Caws will be able to tell you when she has the time.'

His hand disappeared into his trouser pocket. Wide eyed I gazed at the two shilling piece he'd slapped into the palm of my outstretched hand.

I could sense the envious glances around me. Riches beyond measure, four weeks pocket money.

Miss Caws was looking at me in the most affectionate way.

'Weren't you the lad who told me all about Thomas Plumtree when I dropped in to see you after Christmas?'

I nodded to the Canon, but was eager to slip back into oblivion.

'Well Miss Caws, I must be off, well done everyone.' We all stood politely, without being told. Miss Caws was floating.

Thomas Plumtree's name had stuck in my mind ever since I had seen it on a tile on the wall inside the cathedral. His strange name intrigued me so I asked one of the Sisters at the convent and she found a book that told his story. He'd been martyred during the Reformation, put to death for being a priest.

The lads were genuinely amazed at my superior knowledge, they couldn't work out how I'd managed to conjure up the fact. They'd never find out either because I had no intention of telling them.

There wasn't any way that they would find out in the same way that I had because they hardly ever went to Mass on Sunday, let alone spent time long enough to sit and gaze around the walls. I'd known them drop in at the end of Mass to see who was saying Mass, so they could report correctly on the Monday after, when the Mass attendance count was taken. Miss Caws soon became suspicious of the sudden rise in Mass-going and started to ask questions about the sermon. That caught them out. When they couldn't answer she blew up.

'Liars! You will go to hell, you wicked boys, you've soiled your souls. You'll have to tell that in confession, I hope you don't die before you get there.'

Not that they seemed bothered about eternal damnation because their Mass attendances didn't improve. Miss Caws' latest technique on a Monday was to make us close our eyes and put our hands up if we'd been to Mass, relying on implicit honesty. Of course, everyone who had his hand up had a quiet peep to see who the mortal sinners were for the week. She'd do a random selection check afterwards to see if any of the hands raised couldn't answer the questions about the sermon. Failure resulted in the strap. Serving at the convent on a Sunday meant that I always went and being in the choir at the cathedral I had to sing also at High Mass. I never went as far as putting two hands up, but I thought I was justified. I noticed one Sunday when it came to collection time that sometimes parishioners dropped a coin and didn't bother hunting for it, especially if it seemed to roll away. The cathedral was always packed on a Sunday so it would have been difficult to have rummaged around anyway. It gave me an idea, though, so after lunch one Sunday I went back and systematically searched underneath the benches. I ended up with 3/6d plus a gold ring which I dutifully handed in at the presbytery, indicating that I'd just been making a private visit when I noticed it as I had bowed my head in prayer. I didn't mention the 3/6d.

The canon left, Miss Caws visibly relaxed and became buoyant and animated as she declared that we could do whatever we liked till break time as a special treat for answering so well. She caught up with her marking. I was happy to read. It rained. We stayed in, except for a dash to the toilets across the yard and back to a few old, well read, discarded comics that had accumulated in the classroom for wet breaks. Meakin asked for a sweet halfway through. He'd seen me unwrapping one. I took a pineapple chunk out of the bag and threw it over to him at the other side of the classroom. I had aimed wildly high and the individually white wax paper wrapped Buchanan's home-made special pineapple chunk thunked against a glass pane in the partition that separated our room from Mrs Farmer's. The whole class fell instantly silent as they looked towards the glass that had a clearly defined line running diagonally across it. At that precise moment, cue perfect, Mr Monks, the teacher on duty, walked in, looked at the evidence, stared hard at me sheepishly trying to disappear into a hole that failed to materialize and pointed to the door.

'You! Headmaster's room, now! Fast!'

Out I marched to stand and wait. The door opened. The summons came with further pointed finger. The whole incident proceeded like a silent film without the background piano, only the short sharp strapping sound as leather met hand twice, as its own accompaniment.

Explanations were not requested, protestations were similarly unvoiced. The evidence was conclusive, the punishment expected and acceptable for that. The price had to be paid and it was without malice or any further retribution. The affair was closed.

I returned to my class, the silence now a low hum as I entered. The rubbing of hands and the redness of face forestalled any questioning. The rest of the day was trouble free. It needed to be after the peaks and troughs of the morning.

A final weekend reminder about Mass on Sunday as the four o'clock home bell rang out loud and long. We were dismissed quickly.

I was out of the gates and tearing down the lane before the bell had stopped its ringing. I reached the

Essoldo without stopping for breath, even daring the traffic to challenge my journey as I darted out across the roads, twisting through parked cars, people, dustbins, without touching anything or anybody until I had reached Angela. There she was waiting where we'd arranged.

She started to smile when she caught a glimpse of me and that was the nicest touch of the afternoon.

'I'm glad you were able to make it. The doctor was pleased with you?' I panted, hunting for breath as I started to recover from my run.

'Yes. He's given me a clean bill of health as my granny said. I can go back to school on Monday. Hello! It's lovely to see you. You look as if you're ready to burst!'

I was and that's the truth of it, I don't think that I'd ever run quite as fast as that for a long time. Well not since I flew out of our front door, down the path and out the gate, only to see the bus pulling away from the stop. The driver saw me waving but accelerated away, he'd had a hard day no doubt and this was the traditional method of getting back at the world. The passengers watching had a collectively resigned, 'What do you expect?' look about them. I was determined to prove something, so I took off like the wind after the bus, head down, arms bustling and reached the next stop as the last person in the queue was climbing onto the platform. I'd made it, exhausted, but exhilarated. My audience clapped as I dropped into a seat. Thinking about that incident kept me on top for months afterwards.

'I didn't have to make any excuses, my granny wanted me to go to Saddler's the button king for her, so I had a legitimate reason for coming out. She thought it would do me good anyway. I've just arrived.'

I'd recovered my breath and composure.

'I'm glad you're here.'

We walked along side by side, the first time that I'd ever done that of my own free will. It didn't count with my mam, or a partner chosen by Miss Caws. No, this was different, seemed right, but awkward; I didn't know where to put my hands. If it had been one of my mates, my arm would have been round his neck and his round mine as we dragged each other along, regularly breaking free to friendly thump each other. That kind of friendly entanglement clearly didn't apply to this situation. As we walked, my arm swinging freely, occasionally brushed against Angela's arm or hand. I liked that. There didn't seem to be a need either to say sorry for touching her. In normal circumstances I would have been quick to apologize, but this didn't seem normal.

We followed the city walls round to the gate. Angela kept watch while I climbed over. Using my penknife as a screwdriver I removed the screws that held the turned lock. The door pulled open and Angela walked in. I closed the door behind her, took her hand briskly and gently led her over to the hut.

'Close your eyes.' I opened the door and guided her inside.

'Now open them,'

She opened them full and wide, walked over to the stove, sat on it, looking about her, taking in the scene, soaking it up, sponging in the potential.

'I think this is lovely.' There was emotion in her voice as she savoured every word. 'I really do. We could make this so comfortable for ourselves.'

We looked at each other, nodded and said no more.

We sat side by side on the stove, enjoying the peace mingled with a rush of belonging together here, with uncluttered feelings. Outside didn't matter, this was real.

I was the first to break the spell.

'I wonder if we can find any wood.'

Out in the garden there were bits of wood lying around, very damp and not enough to keep a fire going. What we needed were some fruit boxes from the Green Market. I didn't need any excuses. I regularly collected wood to chop into bundles to sell. That supplemented my pocket money. I had regular customers who relied on my top-quality bundles.

The market wasn't far, Angela nodded her approval so I left her behind to her own thoughts as I had mine on the way to the wood. I bought a box of matches and took an old newspaper from a waste bin in Newgate Street before disappearing into the Green Market. I could have had a stack of boxes, but I could only manage four, anyway that would do for the present. On my way back to Angela I bought a bar of chocolate. Food and warmth provided cosily. Living can't be so difficult, can it?

By the time I arrived back the hut had been transformed from an idea to a fact. Angela had cleaned the windows with an old rag, swept the floor with a brush she had discovered in the cupboard and was standing by the stove with one hand on the broom, the other on her hip, suitably poised to say,

'What an asset I am to you!'

'What a fantastic job you've done, you must have moved like a whirlwind.'

She was delighted with the praise and beamed.

Everybody likes praise, properly given. There's not

enough of it.

I laid the fire and lit it. I was a bit worried about the flue and chimney being too dirty with disuse, but I need not have been concerned because before long the fire was well ablaze. The orange box wood mixed well with the old cinders in the grate to bring warmth and glowing red to the hut.

We sat in front of it, my jacket our settee. I opened up the chocolate bar, broke it into its individual pieces and offered a square to Angela. She bit it in half and offered a part to me. We ate. Sweetness. The rest of the bar was consumed in similar ritual fashion. The breaking of food, the sharing of each, self becoming second, each becoming important to the other. We sat after we'd finished eating, watching the silver paper from the chocolate bar fighting among the flames, twisting and turning, shrinking, going black. Black my last memory. Black and cold my wakening. The fire was burnt out, the hut was cold, Angela was lying huddled beside me. I shook her awake gently and gathered myself together.

She stretched long and came together.

'What time is it?'

'I don't know, I've no idea how long we've slept. It must be getting on though. We'd better be getting a move on.'

We struggled to our feet, stiff, bones aching, back sore after the floor and with a last lingering look around we left our hut. We left our walled garden. Screws back in place. I had a feeling I was being watched but couldn't see anyone around. Angel on guard?

'OK, now!'

Me over the wall. Sinclair's clock at the bottom of

Oystershell Lane said half past five, the autumn darkness making the lighted Roman numerals stand out.

We hurried along. I'd be for it, late home, tea spoilt. I'd have to think of a good excuse.

'Angela, it's Saturday tomorrow, why don't we spend the day at our place?

She agreed readily. We parted at her granny's front door and I felt strangely lonely as I made my reluctant way home.

8

Now to face the music. I hadn't thought of an explanation, but I needn't have worried because the house was empty. The back door was open, it always was, whether anybody was in or out. There was a note on the kitchen table. Old Mrs Thompson had died, her son Tommy had called round for my mam to go and lay her out. My mam was always called on to do that job in the neighbourhood. Her mam did it before her, doing the necessary and her mam before that, I vaguely knew what she was called upon to do.

'Somebody's got to do it,' she always said. I suppose so, but it wasn't very pleasant.

My mam wouldn't be pleased to go this time, Tommy had been a conscientious objector, "a conchie," during the war. That was still remembered, but she'd have gone out of sympathy and respect for the old lady who she'd always liked. Tommy was thought by everyone around to have been a plain coward and didn't hold dear the principle of non-aggression at all. I didn't know the truth, only Tommy did and nobody gave him a fair hearing. His family all shied away from him because of it. I wondered if his mother's death would soften people towards him, giving him the benefit of the doubt.

There was some money by the note for some fish and chips. It was a relief that I didn't have to explain my lateness, although it seemed wrong to be relieved as a result of someone's misfortune. Mrs Thompson was past caring, so I don't think she would have minded doing me a favour.

I went out for my supper, I felt I should go to the shop along Sceptre Street instead of the one across the road which was a lot nearer. I didn't know why I should want to go to the other one, but I felt I must, so of course I did.

I decided that I'd have two helpings of chips with plenty of salt and vinegar, but no fish and pocket the difference. I'd fill up with bread and butter if necessary, back home. Chips and pot of tea by the fire. I hurried along to bring the thought nearer to reality. There wasn't a queue, as it was early, so I was straight in and out. The chips freshly made. The heat crept through the paper to warm my hands as I turned for home again. I bumped into my dad.

'Hello son. Where's your mam, there's nobody in the house?'

I told him. He nodded, turned and walked away, his head bowed, his shoulders hunched. It made me feel queasy and unsure for a moment as I watched him go. I noticed that his left heel turned in as he lifted it off the ground, it looked oddly pathetic, it made me sad. I wanted to cry. I wondered what he wanted with my mam.

I had my supper out of the paper, settled in the

armchair by the fire. It was sizzling, red hot, little shafts of gas sprouting out of the coal and bursting into strong red and blue flames, the tar melting into the furnace. After I had finished, I curled up in the leather chair and fell asleep listening to those jets of igniting gas from the coal.

I woke to a smell, before my mam touched me, the sweet smell of death that lingered on her after she returned from a laying out, it seemed to hang around her for days afterwards. I don't know if she used something special when she performed her act of mercy or maybe there was a smell of death that clung and lingered on those living, I was never sure and I didn't want to ask.

'I met my dad when I was at the chip shop. He was looking for you, he didn't say why. I told him where you'd gone.'

She raised her eyes; he hadn't gone round to the Thompson house.

'He doesn't like being near death.'

My mam didn't say any more, but went into the kitchen. I could hear her scrubbing the wooden work tops furiously, I didn't venture in because I sensed that there were other sounds mixed with the scrubbing that were also familiar. I wasn't any use to her, I went upstairs to bed. I wondered if that was something else I shared with my dad.

Saturday was bright, a beautifully warm autumn day.

'This could be the start of an Indian summer,' said our butcher when I took some newspapers over for him. He always gave me a tanner for them. I'd raided my money box before I came out, so with the butcher's money and the returned deposits from some pop bottles I had over a pound. It seemed like a fortune.

My mam was quite happy when I informed her that I was away out. Food was never that important in our house on a Saturday. After a substantial cooked breakfast I could go where I liked as long as I was back before dark. The matinée at the Brighton was my usual first stop, queueing noisily, wondering what could possibly happen to Gene Autrey and how Superman would manage to keep his identity secret for another week and what mad scrapes the Three Stooges would be in for a good laugh. After that it was a bag of chips for lunch, salt and vinegar oozing right through onto my hands, making them warm and somehow reassuring. If it was a match day, I'd meet the lads for a trip to see United. Saturday was always a good day. The best of the week.

I was best out of the house anyway as I always got under my mam's feet and she always wanted me to be helping her about the house, which invariably led to an argument. It would escalate into a full-blown row because I resented being told what to do on a Saturday. I felt restless and wanted to do what I wanted to do. It was my special day, away from the authority restrictions of school and the regulated timetable pattern that my life seemed to fill. I wanted to be allowed to breathe freely without anybody stopping me. I didn't want to go wild, I wanted to be myself, be my own boss, make my own decisions for myself for one day in the week. Saturday was my special day.

My mam accepted that now and did not fight me about it anymore.

Today was different. I was setting out in a new direction but it was still my choice.

United were playing Everton. I'd regret missing that, but I'd decided, so that was unfortunate, but in the changed circumstances unavoidable.

I went immediately round to Angela's. She came straight out almost as soon as I pulled the bell. She was carrying a bag over her shoulder.

'What have you in there?'

'Oh, nothing much, a few bits, some sandwiches, a flask of tea and things.'

We walked quickly down the town, it was almost unbearably difficult not to break into a run, we were so bubbly at the prospect of returning to our place behind the walls for the first full day together.

We didn't speak at all as we walked, but listened to the sound of our footsteps as they mingled with the Saturday shoppers in town. It wasn't long before we reached the door in the wall, but it was ages before the coast was clear. There were so many people about, we decided to keep walking up and down so as not to draw attention to ourselves. Then for a moment everything was still, nobody was in sight, I was up and over the wall in a flash, had the door open, Angela in, the door screwed up shut, the walk across the dewy grass, sparkling in the sharp sun, a lovely day. When we opened the door and stepped inside, I stood, not really sure what to do, but Angela had direction, she burst into action. There she was busying herself, tidying around, opening windows, sweeping up. I lit the fire, then went out to search for more fuel. There was a tarpaulin pulled over a mound of something at the far end of the garden against the wall. I had noticed it before, but not investigated. I did now. I pulled back the sheet to reveal a mountain of neatly stacked tarry toots, the name we gave to old wooden street cobbles soaked in tar. They burned hot and long. It was possible to buy them from the local corporation when they resurfaced the roads, lifting the old cobbles which were more suited to horse drawn transport, gentler on the horses hooves and quieter under the wheel of the wagons, all long gone.

I was ecstatic with my find. Here was our ready supply of fuel, there was enough to last for weeks if necessary. Weeks! A joyous, reckless thought. With two armfuls I returned to our hut, leaving some neatly stacked outside the door in true pioneer fashion. I threw one on the fire. It sizzled as it burned the rich pitch and wood, creating a powerful homely heat and luxuriant aroma.

There was a red blanket on the floor, glowing brighter in reaction to the fierce light.

'Where did that come from?'

'I found it at my granny's.'

'But I didn't see you bring it. It wasn't in your bag was it? I would have noticed something so bulky.'

She smiled and started to giggle.

'I watched my granny dressing herself the other day by the fire and I noticed that she always wraps herself in a blanket before she pulls on her dress, fastening it with an enormous safety pin. So I did the same!'

Well I had to laugh.

'How did you manage that? Tell me please do!'

Angela was delighted that I hadn't noticed and warmed to her explanation.

'It was a right struggle to get into my dress, but I managed in the end and with my overcoat on nobody noticed I was a size or two larger. Well you didn't.'

'You're right, I didn't, I'd never have guessed. Or maybe I was too much of a gentleman to suggest you'd put on weight.'

She didn't know whether to take me seriously until she saw me smile.

'Oh you!' She squealed, thumping me gently on the arm. I keeled over feigning pain and we both started laughing as I righted myself next to her on the blanket by the stove. Somehow the laughter changed to a chuckle, then a gurgle to a hum, a hum of a tune we both knew, it was something we sang at school regularly, 'Lord for to-morrow and its needs I do not pray...' It captured our mood, it cast its spell 'just for to-day,' on a red carpet island surrounded by four warm walls, outside a sea of green, the city walls of long ago, but strong, protective. There's a strength behind those walls. We are that strength. They hide us, have given us a place where we belong. Protect us, keep us safe as long as we remain. Spirits of the past hover above, looking down, casting their shadows, throwing their dreams through time to us now. In my reverie, I catch a faint smell of strawberries and the old Dominican slips into my head.

'Let's stay here forever,'

Angela looked at me through my eyes and nodded sagely.

'Forever and a day.'

We remained sitting till we'd hummed away our tune, 'Just for today...'

'What do we do about a toilet?' The spell broken. 'I noticed that there wasn't one.'

'Well we'll do what they do out in the wilds, the grass round the back of the hut for one, and it's secluded and I'll dig a hole for the other. It'll make the flowers grow!'

I was surprised at myself for even saying something like that. I'd never really thought of a girl going to the toilet before, it didn't feel quite right, but Angela was so matter of fact and natural about it all, it seemed so normal, practical and quickly dismissed, problem solved and forgotten. Well not quite forgotten, often when the conversation turns to toilets the need suddenly arrives. I wasn't embarrassed at all even though I realized the sound would carry through the window. I washed my hands at the tap and dried them on my pullover. When I returned the blanket was spread out with sandwiches and the flask of tea.

We ate our meal slowly, deliberately, savouring every mouthful. Egg and tomato sandwiches had never tasted so good. The tea was hot, sweet and strong. We had to share the flask top as a cup, the only one we had. I liked sharing. I was glad it was all we had.

We talked and talked. I'd never have believed that I could have enthused about curtains, furniture, cooking meals. It was all a long way from scoring an equalizing goal in the dying seconds of a football match. Whatever would the lads think of me if they heard me now? I certainly wouldn't live it down. I didn't care what they thought. I'm me, that's important.

The day flew by, I wondered what the lads would think if they knew. We went to all the games together, rarely missed, unless at death's door. If we didn't have the money we helped each other over the wall to sneak in for free. They'd be wondering where I was. We'd beaten Everton four-nil earlier in the year, but it was never usually an easy game with them.

I explained all this to Angela.

'Do you want to go?'

'No really, I'm happy here, I'll listen to the sounds

coming from the ground. It's just over there, we're really close.'

A few oohs and aahs, but only one great roar. Maybe we'd won one-nil. I hoped so. Everybody in the city would be happy tonight. Perhaps.

We played cards. I had a miniature pack that I always carried with me. I won them at the Hoppings, throwing a wooden ball into an angled bucket without it jumping out. We played rummy, it was the only card game I knew, apart from snap. A St. John of God religious brother taught me when he stayed with us one weekend. He was visiting the churches to preach about the work of the order and to ask for donations. He was a gentle, jovial old Friar Tuck-like character who I'd watched on Robin Hood, with snuff stains all down the front of his habit. He gave me some snuff once. It nearly blew my head off as I sneezed and sneezed. He laughed to the rhythm of my explosions and his belly shook wildly. He enjoyed a game of rummy, we played with broken matchsticks. He always chuckled when he won as he gathered up his winnings. He didn't have any money of his own and it was something he never talked about.

I explained the rules to Angela, remembering the words Brother Richard used and the stages of his teaching me the game. I think I taught her well because we had a long, happy game with each winning some. We didn't play for matchsticks and it didn't matter.

I laid the cards aside to a gathering warm stillness surrounding us. Angela took a thin book from her bag, it was small, leather bound, she opened it and started to read.

'I watched you to-day
Sitting in our love

And smiled awhile
To think of us
Encased in an egg
Unbreakable -
Except from within.'

She read it again, closed the book and carefully slid it back in her bag. She didn't say anything about it. It was meant to be left there.

We continued to sit, watching the fire stirring again in the stove as the tarry toots began to bubble and burst into flames. It was safe enough to have the door open and they didn't spark. I went out for some more. The afternoon was wearing on to evening with a chill in the air. I gathered up the cobbles in an orange box. They stacked nicely and took a large amount, and returned to the hut, shivering as I closed the door behind me.

'It's really chilly out there, the day's disappearing fast for us. We're going to have to make a decision soon.'

The unspoken had finally been given its shape. An important decision was looming, it was there moving up on us as the darkness crept out of the day to smother it.

'Are we really intending to stay here? What will my mam think and your gran, they'll be worried sick.'

'Let's sit and think this through.'

We sat. The fire grew and fell. As the darkness came from the firelight, the picture became clearer. It came reaching from the starkness.

'What's out there to compare with what we have here?'

'Who's really that concerned about either of us?'

'Your granny?'

'True, she does care, but I interfere with her life.

She's too old, she can't be bothered, she'd sooner I wasn't staying there. Look at the trouble I've caused already with the air raid shelter accident. It's too much of a strain for her, she doesn't need it or deserve it. And my mam and dad, they don't care. My granny rang my dad about the accident. I don't think he was bothered once he knew I was alright. I haven't heard from him or my mam. They're too busy wrapped up in themselves to notice anybody else. Well I think it's time for me now. I want to stay here. I don't want to go from here. And what about you? Tell me who is concerned about you?'

She was right, nobody appeared to care about her out there. Here was different, it couldn't be measured like that, we were for each other in some way. And me? Who cared for me?

'My mam in her own way. She cares, I suppose, but I'm too much for her on her own and not enough as well. I remind her too much of my dad and that hurts her and fires her up as well. She lives her own life mostly lost in her own thoughts. She's a lost cause to herself and me, I'd not be greatly missed. There's never a show of tenderness or affection. I'd like to stay and make it last.'

Turning to face each other simultaneously clasping hands within hands it was solemnly agreed, a pact to remain. Cemented further with the briefest of hugs.

9

'We'll need food. I've just over a pound.' I'd been saving up.

'The market will be packing up, so the chances of bargains are high, they don't like hanging on to stuff over the weekend.'

'I have half a crown, so we should be able to stock up a bit if we're careful. If we could find something to boil water in, we'd be able to have tea, coffee and soup.'

'Look, I'll tell you what. If you go and buy us some food stuff, I'll find stuff to cook with.'

That agreed, we left the hut, making sure that the fire was well happed up, then we made our way across the grass and out through the door.

'I'll leave it open, but closed, I don't think anyone will come by. Be sure no one sees you when you come back.'

Reluctantly we separated, I felt a pang and saw a hesitation in Angela before she gathered herself and was off down the narrow road by the walls, she looked fragile against the roughly hewn and weathered stone.

I turned off and into the main street to become caught up in the throng of football supporters as they surged towards bus and train station or parked cars from St. James' Park. The atmosphere was lively.

'Hey Mister, what was the score?'

'Two-one.'

'Who to?'

'Everton. Wor Jackie wasn't playing and we missed him.'

So it wasn't surprising that I had only heard one great roar, there was never much enthusiasm when the opposition banged one in, or as in this case two. The away side's fans' cheers never carried very far.

An idea came to me and I followed it up immediately. A number of cars were parked nearby. I casually strolled up beside them looking purposeful and waited. I stood glancing round as someone approached, stamping my feet a bit and blowing into my hands. A couple wearing their black and white scarves neared me.

'Hello Missus, Mister, I've minded your car all through the match. I stopped some lads from scratching it, little tearaways. I sharp chased them, you should have seen them run. They didn't come back, mind they wouldn't would they with me keeping guard?'

The man gave me a knowing look.

'No I suppose they wouldn't,' as he dipped his hand into his pocket. I helped the lady in at her side and gently closed the door.

'Nice car Mister, thank you. Will you be here for the next match? It's against Portsmouth. I'll keep this space for you, we'll likely win that one.'

'Aye, alright then, that'll be just grand.'

A few more coppers in my pocket, what a great result, for me, us. Five more satisfied customers coughed up. It would have been more if we'd won.

It usually stayed with me when we'd lost, but not today as I rushed to the shops before they closed.

A pan, some cutlery and a few other bits from the hardware shop, just catching it open. Nothing great, but paid for with hard earned cash, not quite honest, not quite begging, enterprising, tradition, preferable to stealing.

Acting is worth its own reward and more, better for my sensitive conscience. I made my way back to the hut, a little paradise, pleased with myself, reliving my audacity as I strode along with my purchases neatly wrapped with brown paper under my arm. I was eager to see how Angela was doing in our hideaway home. I refused to allow anyone to break the spell. I felt that I was separate breezing briskly through the streets focused on my simple task. If I'd met someone I knew I don't think they would have been able to see me.

I was home before Angela. The place was cosy. I filled the pan with water from the tap in the garden and placed it on top of the stove, it gleamed, shining, new. The cutlery laid out on the blanket. Well done kind United fans.

'How on earth did you manage to buy all that?' were Angela's first words as she hurried through the door and spied everything.

I delighted in re-telling the story, gathering momentum as I went along, responding extravagantly to the laughs and gasps of amazement and joy and her little claps of delight at my audacity and cheek.

Angela meanwhile had bought well, grasping at every bargain she could find. She'd had to shop before with little, so she knew how to win.

We settled back with a flask of coffee and the single cup, eating our deliciously succulent Dickman's steak and kidney pies, the best that money could buy, listening to the sounds of our eating above the crackling stove. Neatly cut slices of cheese to follow with cream crackers lightly buttered, then an apple each and a couple of chocolate biscuits each. A substantial meal, two satisfied and relaxed bodies, little washing up. The balance right.

'I'll wash, if you dry!'

The smile. The ritual washing at the tap, the drying by the fire, the tidying up, the orderly peace. Not a cross word anywhere.

The darkness had fully descended now. The night sky was crisp, clear, the stars bright in the above. We closed the door and lay in front of the fire on our blanket, red and extra warming. The firelight danced off the walls and ceiling, telling its stories in the darkness, the fire now in charge and the only sound, the pictures wide and vivid. We didn't talk, but lay allowing the warm, soft glow to drift into our essence. I thought I saw someone looking in at the window, I was prone to that, so I didn't bother to move from my comfortable spot and check. If it was, we'd know soon enough. We must have lain for ages, because the fire started to lose its stories, then its heat.

I put on more tarry toots, I wished for potato peelings to cover the burning so that it would last the night, keeping us warm. I felt responsible. I understood fires, it was down to me to maintain our warmth, it was our security. I geared myself to wake and feed the stove. I organized my mind to waking to the near dying embers, content that we'd no need to worry, we settled ourselves to sleep.

'Goodnight Angela.'

'Goodnight.'

We lay on the blanket with it rolled over us so that we were snug together, wrapped tightly to keep ourselves in and everything else, cold, the world, out. We touched hands and brushed faces, turned and drifted off, off in our cocoon, heads resting heavily on carefully folded overcoats.

I woke suddenly. Angela was asleep, pressed against my back. The darkness was intense at first. I felt myself desperately trying to find sight. Eventually I focused on the slight glow remaining in the grate, I calmed, my equilibrium restored. Well done lad, you've woken in time, as you said, before the fire died, stir yourself and fill up the stove.

I stretched long, I felt stiff from the hard bed, I shifted slightly from Angela, but clumsily and she began to stir as I packed up the fire. I was annoyed with myself for having woken her. I'd wanted to do my job and creep back under the blanket, undetected, to drift back to sleep beside the growing firelight. It hadn't worked. We were both wide awake.

'Would you like some cheese and milk?'

'Only if we can leave the dishes till the morning.'

I had to smile, there was still a place for jokes, even at this uncomfortable hour.

'All right then, lazybones!'

I broke off a couple of pieces of cheese and we drank from the cup, the milk tasted sweet.

'I'll make some toast, it seems a shame to waste the red glow.'

A piece of stick served as a toasting fork, the sound and luscious aroma of toasting bread before a hot stove, mingling with the tarred wood was magical.

'I like nothing better than a piece of toast thickly spread with butter and a glass of cold milk by an open fire late at night with a good book to read.'

'That sounds lovely, we have it all, even the book.'

The butter dribbled down the toast and onto our lips. Angela hunted out her little leather-bound book. She stopped and turned to me.

'Never mind the book, you're better company.'

I stared at her.

'Blow out the candle, fuse the lights
Let no one know what lurks to-night
Creep into a corner there to wait
For sense to let you know your fate.'

'Why did you suddenly say that?'

'I don't know, it came out of me.'

'That's strange.'

We'd finished eating and snuggled closer together, needing each other. We were about settled, easy with ourselves, when I had the strangest feeling again that we were being watched. The strength of the emotion was intense. I could feel the eyes deep into us. I turned my head. There wasn't anybody in the hut, the darkened window showed stars without any hindrance. Nothing. I rolled off the blanket and stood up. Angela must have sensed something too because she was up beside me, holding onto me tight. Together we walked slowly over to the window and peeped out.

There was somebody walking about on the grass around the edge of the walls. Angela clung to me more closely, I could feel her heart pounding, matching mine. She started to shake.

'It's alright, don't be frightened, we won't be harmed, there isn't any danger, you've no need to worry.' I felt myself hearing those words without having thought them first. The words came and I listened as well. They weren't mine. Angela relaxed, we rubbed the glass and looked more closely, shading our eyes with hands moulded into blinkers to cut out the light from the hut.

The figure appeared shadowy in white long flowing robes, suddenly caught in the moonlight underneath a black wraparound cloak with hood. The head turned. The light revealed a gaunt white face, lips moving. A man, his eyes sunken far back were reaching towards his open hands holding a book. He was reading from his book as he moved, gliding along over the grass in unfettered motion towards the hut, towards us. He was coming our way. As he approached, we stood still, transfixed, lost in the moment, unable to change course, our direction firmly held. He stopped. Out of the depths there tolled the doleful single note of a distant bell.

'Listen to the bell as we pass it by.
Does it ring out for you and I?'

He looked up from his reading and gazed into us, his eyes gave meaning to his movement. There was a softness, an asking, a smile, deep inside. His gaze returned to his book, hunched. He continued his journey round the walls. We continued our involvement as we watched. When he reached the far end he turned, opened his arms to us, smiled again and walked through the wall.

He was older, there weren't any strawberries offered, the smile was the same, I recognized him.

The walls, the grass, the hut and we remained still.

Night returned to us, the stars shone through, the fire sparkled behind us.

'I want to go home.' Angela had removed her dress and was standing in her knickers socks and vest, hurriedly, frantically wrapping the red blanket round and around herself, safety pin firmly held between her lips, her face white.

I slowly reached out and took her arm.

'Don't go,' I told her. 'You don't have anything to worry about. I'm sure of that, he doesn't mean us any harm. I've seen him before. Didn't you see him smile? There wasn't any malice in his face. We are safe here. Trust me. Really, we are alright. Please stay.'

She stopped what she was doing and allowed the pin to drop from her lips. I could feel the calmness returning to her. Suddenly she smiled, confident that she could rely on me for her safety. I felt very strong and grown up. I was of importance, wanted by someone who trusted me implicitly. I felt more wanted now than I'd ever been before.

She dropped her blanket onto the floor again and was embarrassed to see me looking at her without her dress. She looked up, giggled a bit and put her dress back on. Modesty restored, she faced me.

'Come on, let's snuggle down, it must be very late and we need our sleep.'

I obliged, settling myself in front of the fire beside her, wrapped in our togetherness.

'I think I recognized what he was. It looked like he was wearing a friar's habit and I think he was reading his breviary.'

'How do you know that?'

'I remember having to serve Mass at the convent for a priest dressed like that. He was a Dominican, the brother of one of the nuns there. He'd been invited to her silver jubilee. I remember being impressed with his black and white habit. He was really pleasant. He told me that it was a Dutch Dominican priest who'd organized the East and West End football teams to amalgamate and become United and that's why they wear black and white. I don't know if it's true. The friar outside was dressed exactly the same.'

'But who was that outside? Why did he come right up to us and smile at us and then again open his arms wide to us before he disappeared *through* the wall? What does he want from us?'

'I don't know, I can't answer your questions, but I felt a comfort in his smile and I realized we were safe, no matter what. Didn't you sense something?'

'Not until you talked to me about it all. I was frightened. I've never experienced anything like that. I mean you could hardly call it normal!'

'Certainly not normal, but what is normal. Is this? Perhaps we'll have to let normal disappear from our thinking and allow ourselves to be carried along with the events.'

Angela had succumbed to the heat and sleep and drowsiness crept over me as well. I wondered if he approved of us here. I felt peaceful when he smiled. There was protection there, something wholesome and strong. The walk around us, encircling us with his blessing. I dropped off, wondering if Thomas Plumtree had paid us a visit, but I quickly rejected that as I knew he hadn't been a Dominican. Sleep came comfortably. I'd not slept close to anyone since I was a toddler and I couldn't remember that. I didn't have any brothers or sisters and my mam used to push me out of her bed if I sneaked in for a cuddle at the weekend, after my dad left. I felt so relaxed and comforted by the presence of someone next to me, the sound of her breathing, her breath against my head. That feeling of belonging was the last I remember of the night.

10

I awoke alert and well refreshed, despite the disturbances of the night. I jumped up. It was the first time that I'd ever been able to do that. As I woke, I could see everything so clearly. It was as if I had woken up into the day but catching the hidden mysteries of night unawares as I did so, taking with me the knowledge of the darkness. I felt that I understood what life was all about, what the world meant, the great vast mysteries of infinity no longer remained secret. I knew where I was going, the purpose of my every act, my place in the jigsaw of existence. I had solved the problems of the universe, I understood eternity and forever. Omniscience came with the blinding clarity of wakening and the reality of knowing limited it, slowly closing in on it, bringing it to an end, the finite darkness. I fought desperately to retain it, plunging my mind back into the black hole that has light, but my mind realized the futility of it and refused to go.

I stood by the window where there was evidence of a frost, the glass clouded with its cold patterns. I cleared part and looked out, the grass was stiff, crisp, white. I half expected to see footprints circling the wall, but wasn't surprised when I didn't. I followed the wall round as the praying friar had walked. My journey stopped. Incredible! Where the friar had disappeared from our view was a bricked-up postern, its shape clearly discernible. The old carefully constructed design moulded strong with younger bricks stuffed in to fill a tedious gap. A blocked-up doorway. That must have led somewhere, but where?

I turned away from my thoughts and to morning to gaze down at Angela. She was still fast asleep, lying snugly wrapped in her blanket, her hands joined under the side of her head. She looked as if she hadn't a worry in the world, and here, that was true. I'd care for her. A picture of her flashed into my mind standing before me half-clothed, embarrassed. Poor Angela. I began to feel sentimental and emotional. I was glad she didn't wake to see me wipe my eyes on my sleeve. I continued to gaze, my mind's eye focusing carefully upon her, photographing her peaceful simplicity to be retained inside me forever.

I lit the fire as quietly as I could, cleaning out the accumulated ash and discovering the last remaining burning, faintly glowing embers beneath the grey waste. A well-placed tarry root and she was blazing. I didn't want to wake the sleeper, but I needed to walk. I found a pencil stub among my cluttered possessions and wrote on the brown wrapping paper.

'Just slipped out for a stroll. Don't fret, will be back soon. Love.'

The city felt fresh in the early morning frost. It was early too, half past something or other according to the Northern Goldsmith's clock. I didn't quite see exactly, because my eyes travelled up to the golden naked lady stretched on tiptoe, arms out wide, unashamedly expansive above the clock piece. I tried not to look at her, as we'd been told at school that it was wicked, a sin to look at, a soul staining act that would require forgiveness in confession. It was difficult to narrow my eyes to avoid her and only see the figures on the clock face alone. I gave up, uncomfortably shaking my shoulders as I walked on by. What's important about the time anyway, there's no hurry for anything.

I picked up some discarded newspapers from the litter bins. I spied the Football Pink and rested by Cowen's monument to read the report on the big match. Jackie Milburn had been sorely missed. I'd missed a poor game by all accounts, so for once reading about it was quite sufficient. I pictured our goal being scored anyway and let out a great roar, 'GOAL!' full voice and came to wondering what Joseph Cowen made of it all standing there on his plinth above where I was sitting. He wasn't saying anything and there wasn't anyone else abroad at this early hour to hear me.

There was a peacefulness about the streets, the trolley buses hadn't started their soft hum around the city. I stuffed the newspapers in my pockets, they'd do if I let the fire go out. A couple of railwaymen in their uniforms were walking in unison to the early shift, bait bags slung casually over their slumped shoulders, nobody to upbraid them now, cigarettes glowing from their lips. I hid behind a corporation workmen's hut as they approached. They didn't see me I was sure. I suddenly felt the need to remain hidden. Our absence would surely have been discovered by now and I didn't want anyone to see me alone in the city at this early bird hour on a Sunday morning. It would surely arouse anyone's suspicions. Carefully I made my way back to the hut unnoticed.

My note had been unnecessary as Angela was still sleeping. I left her lying as my thoughts turned to food. I slipped out and filled the pan with water and put it on the stove. I cleaned out the flask and put coffee in it, waiting patiently for the water to boil. It's true what they say.

Eventually the gentle bubbling up caused Angela to wake.

'Hello love, breakfast is almost ready. Did you sleep well?'

She wriggled and stretched long and gloriously into wakefulness, looking content. She was refreshed despite the disturbances in the night.

'Coffee, bread, cheese, fruit, biscuit, OK?'

'Sounds delicious!'

And so it proved.

During our meal the memory of the night crept back to us.

What had we both seen? A restless friar? Perhaps that, but more we could not say. I was sure that we'd find out when the time was right. As we finished eating and musing we became a bit maudlin, the reality of our situation creeping through even though we tried to stop it. I realized why I had woken so early on a Sunday. I should have been somewhere else. Oh well. I finished munching the last piece of biscuit, broken and shared,

'For you.'

'We haven't a lot of food left you know, enough for today and maybe tomorrow, but as well there isn't much money. I want to stay, but I don't see how we can.'

Angela stiffened and was defiant.

'Let's not talk about it, let's be for now and let the waters flow until they're stopped.'

She didn't know where the words had come from, but their power helped me. We decided to act normally, forget the problems and vowed to remain undetected as long as possible.

I watched Angela wash at the tap, shivering with the cold then rush back to the fire to be wrapped round dry with the blanket. When she was comfortably dried it was my turn. I stripped down to my underpants and rushed out, the frost bit into my feet as I pounded over to the tap. The icy torrent stung my face and body as I splashed it over me. I was like a soaking, melting ice-block by the time I ran full pelt back to the fire, shivering and shaking until I felt the warmed blanket wrapped around me and gentle hands to rub me dry. I felt a double warm glow outside and in with those soft hands.

After we'd dressed and laid the blanket in front of the fire to dry we went outside to our walled garden and I pointed out where the friar had turned from us and disappeared. I felt the bricks. They had been solidly in place for generations. There were no other exits from the garden except for our door.

'I wonder who he was?'

'Where was he going?'

'Where did he come from?'

And together we looked and said,

'And what does he want?' Angela adding, 'With us.'

There were no answers.

I closed my eyes and invited Angela to do likewise.

I held her hand and placed her other one with mine against the wall. We walked slowly around, following the night journey of the friar, absorbing the walls as we moved, investigating every crack and crevice, every bump and deviation, every mason's mark of ownership, fingering the life gone and the crumbling weather dust that surfaced.

In my darkness I pictured a garden rich with flowers, birds and trees, a hot day, the colours sparkling in the sun's gift to us. The sweet welcoming smells of summer. There was a stone-slabbed walkway, with friars, softly padding their way round, silent except for the swing of beads against their habits and hum of whispered prayer. When each had finished they took rest awhile on roughly hewn seats, some of stone, some cleverly drawn from fallen trees, there apart, scattered in a peaceful space, enjoying the high warmth and inbuilt calm, rejoicing in tranquil luxury.

Afterwards, as the sun began to pass away, they gathered their black cloaks around them, threw up their hoods and moved away to disappear through the postern and take their places once more in the friary and the outside world.

'Angela what do you see?'

'Trees, overgrown paths, broken down gateways and buildings in ruin.'

'I think you are centuries ahead of me.'

The spell was broken and we let go of each other's hand, but not immediately.

I needed to run, round and round the garden, through the ages. Off I went, zigzagging over the grass, forward, rolling, kicking, jumping, skipping, hopping, bouncing off the extremities, turning and running back again. Angela, caught up in my frenzy, joined in as we curled and weaved our patterns over the whitened grass, like so many snails on a moonlit venture carving their various trails as they journeyed some place. The panting, the pounding, the exhilaration, the exhaustion, collapsing in a heap, spent, but only for Angela to collapse on top of me and pin my arms down with her legs. I struggled to free myself and was surprised to find that I couldn't. She was like a dead weight upon me. I thought something had happened because she appeared very still. I struggled and struggled as my confidence began to ebb into humiliation at the hands of a slightly built young girl. She laughed suddenly and relieved, I managed to catch her unawares and rolled her off. The split second loss of focus had weakened her resolve and gave me my chance. We rolled and rolled together, oblivious of the state of the ground, holding on, gathering momentum, on top, under, over, close together, embraced, laughing, heads touching, face, hair, arms, bodies, legs entwined. Close. Then totally collapsed. Stopped, but for the panting, panting, slowing to a calm.

I lifted my head and propped it up on my hand.

'You're great, you, I enjoyed that. D'you know something, you're fun to be with. I've never said that to a... a girl before. You're somehow different from the rest. I can't figure it out. You have a kind of sparkle.'

Angela looked and beamed at me, I was embarrassed and was about to bury my head into the grass when she tweaked my nose with her thumb and finger, pretending that she'd captured it and said,

'Don't look so serious then!' And proceeded to roll back across to our hut.

I watched her go over and round and suddenly felt sad.

She appeared so small in the grass, with the tracks we had created.

I stood up slowly and walked back to the hut, unsure of myself.

We bustled about the hut, drying off quickly and arranging our few possessions in order, the fire blazing, our blanket toasty in front of it, our bed, our settee, our table, our magic carpet.

With everything tidy, we left the hut. If the fire died while we were out we could easily relight it on our return.

After taking the necessary precautions against being spotted, we left the garden.

11

On Sunday the Quayside was alive with all manner of stalls, entertainment, noise, hustle and bustle, perfect to become anonymous in, but to enjoy ourselves at the same time. A fish and chip stall would provide our lunch and later we'd visit the cathedral to hunt for stray coins.

We went by a public toilet on our way there, looked knowingly at each other and took the opportunity. Then we made our way down Dog Leap Stairs. They were steep and plenty.

'Do you know Angela, my great-great-granddad is supposed to have ridden down here on horseback. I think he was drunk at the time, pretending to be Dick Turpin and about to hold somebody up!'

'Gosh, it hardly seems possible, they're so steep, he must have been a fine horseman even if he was drunk."

'When he had sobered up and my great-great-granny told him what he had done he went white, shivered and was violently sick before taking to his bed for a week!'

We laughed at the thought. I popped into a newsagent's and bought the *Sunday Sun*. There wasn't any news about us in it, our apparent disappearance must still be largely unknown. We might not even be linked together, although the police must have pieced together that likelihood.

'Oh dear.'

'What's wrong?'

I had spied some more information about the bishop and his housekeeper and instantly remembered the promise I had made. Never mind, the nuns would survive without another cutting from me. They'd be wondering where I was though, not turning up to serve Mass for them. We should go to Mass, but I couldn't see how that was possible. Somebody would recognize me and that would be the end for us. But missing Mass on a Sunday knowingly was dreadful. I didn't know how my conscience was going to cope with that.

'Nothing much, just a promise I can't keep. It's not very important. Perhaps it's as well. I don't think I should have promised in the first place.'

We were a little more confident that our disappearance wasn't widely known, it meant we could relax.

And so to the Quayside.

It was busy and the Salvation Army band was standing under the bridge, canopied by large sheets. Painters above were at work, cleaning up the kittiwake nests, de-rusting, painting while the Army brassed out its Sunday message of hope. A rattling can beating out perfect time to the music was moving through the crowd. There's always a collection. A lost soul was heavily at work, head close to the pavement as he brought his art forms to life, a cap with a few coppers in it beside his chalks. Angela added to it. The artist briefly acknowledged her. A French onion seller cycled along, his onions tied and draped down either side of his bicycle.

'Did he cycle all the way from France?'

'I think so. What a life.'

The smell from his deeply smoked cigar wafted past us. I turned and gathered in the rich aroma, noticing a policeman on his patrol, looking out for skullduggery of any kind. I grabbed Angela's arm and we moved smartly towards a crowd caught up in the patter of an Indian tradesman selling blankets, sheets and towels.

'Come over, white trash, bloody English, come and get cheated by a daft Indian.'

His pseudo abusive banter with the crowd brought laughter, joviality, many sales and no offence. The mood was friendly and warm, feelings mutually kind. He was as local as his customers. The policeman had moved on so we continued on our way.

There were animals for sale, dogs, cats, birds, rabbits, the sight of them caged up depressed us before we caught the smell of their fear. We didn't stop to look.

An old man, drip hanging from his nose and gathering momentum to fall, was selling jumping beans, multicoloured and leaping all over his wooden tray. They looked funny. I was waiting for one to be bombed by a falling drip. We laughed as I whispered. There were puppets for sale. French poodles looking real as they walked along the pavement, their heads bobbing up and down, legs lightly mincing along.

'Come on ladies and gentlemen, buy your pets here. Guaranteed house trained, you don't have to worry about stains on the carpet. Very obedient. Extremely cheap to a good home.'

Amazingly alive looking, lots of people stood transfixed by their dainty movements. What a buy they would be. I'd have had one myself if I'd had the money to spare, but we strolled on.

A large circle of spectators were being entertained by a man being tied up in chains. Four soldiers volunteered to do the job and now they went about it. The man, barefooted and wearing only trousers, braced himself and tensed his muscles till the veins stood out as the soldiers wrapped the chains around him. His hands were tied, chains around his neck, between his legs, round his chest, his arms, his back, he looked secured. An assistant thanked the soldiers and padlocked the chain to make certain it wouldn't come loose. The soldiers slapped their hands, delighted, as they returned to the crowd, certain that he would never free himself.

'Let's see the bugger get out of that!'

The showman shouted over to them, almost choking out the words.

'Wait a minute, lads! You're not finished yet.'

The soldiers stopped and turned back to him, their looks said it all. What more could he want?

'Just want you to make a proper job of it. Lift me into that sack and throw me into the Tyne.'

The four soldiers stared at him as if he'd gone mad. The crowd were hushed still, only the occasional chink of chain as the tied man swayed. The soldiers reluctantly returned and pulled the sack over him, the crowd opened into a semi-circle as they carried their human load to the edge of the Quay and with swinging movement, on the count of three released him out into the cold murky waters.

The semi-circle quickly became a deep line as everybody moved closer to the edge and looked down. I started counting in thousands, each one thousand the equivalent of a second. The ripples spread across the oily waters and the time grew longer. The nervous murmurs in the crowd needed no translation, the uncomfortable shufflings as some people turned to go. Angela came closer to me, the soldiers looking concerned, their former banter silenced. One looked ready to dive in.

Suddenly with the force of a ball from a cannon, the escape artist shot through. He surfaced, sack in one hand, chains in the other, arms outstretched to accept the roars of the crowd. Over he swam to the steps and mounted them, the returning hero, enjoying the genuine delighted applause of a relieved and astounded crowd. His circle returned as he entered it, dripping, shiny patches of oil clinging to him, water pooling at his feet.

He sat down, he'd no more to say, his act was complete. A silver coin landed beside him, then another and another until there was a crescendo of falling coins at his feet, landing in the puddle he'd formed. One coin came rolling towards me and I smartly trapped it under an alert foot. A quick bend and a quicker movement of the hand and a sixpence was resting snugly in the palm. I handed it to Angela. It's unlucky to keep a sixpence you have found. It should always be given to someone you care about. She smiled at me, then threw it back towards the man. I took her hand.

'You're right,'

Someone further on, remarkably like the drenched body recently risen from the Tyne was spelling out how he intended to swallow ten feet of chain. His voice was raw as he spoke and he found breathing difficult, bending almost double as he took breath, his neck muscles outstanding as he heaved in the Quayside air. He picked up the stainless chain and began to swallow one link at a time, all eyes on him.

'Where's it all going?'

On he went, relentlessly pursuing his goal until nothing remained showing except one solitary link. He held it tightly between his lips, then struck a long match, intently watching the chemical burn off before shaking it dead. He put the spent match vertically through the final link, forming a barrier and so preventing it from slipping into his mouth and down his throat to join the rest of its companions.

Walking round his audience, he invited people by gesture to feel his stomach, towards one side. He moved towards us, smelling violently of heavy sweating, snatched my hand and forced it against himself. There was an unmistakable feel of solid pieces of metal resting together, there inside him. It was the oddest sensation, sending a shiver up my spine.

After his slow procession, he returned to the centre of his pitch, picked up a towel, withdrew the matchstick from the last visible link, held the towel to his mouth and in a process of regurgitation and simulated vomiting he started to bring up the chain from his stomach, little by little out into the towel, doubling up in a stiff jerking action as he proceeded. With a powerful, painful primitive growl, the whole chain up out and lying before us on the towel, wet with sweat, saliva, and frothing gastric matter. With arms tensed slightly apart from his side, fingers pointing downwards towards his chain he waited for our response. It came in a flourish and he was pleased, the coins were still clattering towards him as we continued on our way.

The joke man had a tap fixed to his forehead. He was extolling the virtues of a whoopee cushion while watching a group of lads eyeing his merchandise. He turned aside to them, from the corner of his mouth,

'If you lift anything, I'll have you, believe me!'

Smiling he engaged with his audience with hardly a pause and threw a jar of ink over a lady's white blouse. Her face matched the colour as she looked down at the splodge. She was about to explode when the stain miraculously started to disappear and quickly became invisible. That was something. The lady received a free gift. Lots of people spent their money. We left the stall.

'So this is how you spend your Sundays?'

'With all the church I go to I need the balance.'

'Do you think our friar would have had this in his day?'

'I'm sure it would have been equally as varied and as entertaining - and food. I'm hungry, my mouth is beginning to water.'

The unique smell of fish and chips caught our enthusiasm and we hurried along. We had to wait in a queue, it was always popular. It just meant when we sat down to eat we savoured every mouthful, the golden-coloured and wildly shaped chips were cooked to perfection, the vinegar, the salt. The batter crisp and mellow, breaking into the brilliant white flesh of the gift from the sea.

'Only thing missing, bread and butter and a pot of tea.'

But we weren't complaining.

We sauntered back along the Quayside as the

crowds began to thin. The stall holders were starting to gather up their wares, the Salvation Army band had gone off for lunch, the pavement artist's work was being trodden on, not maliciously, lost in the throng of families hurrying home to their Sunday roast, happy at time well spent together. There was more evidence of policemen about, checking that the stalls were closed and gone by two o'clock.

'We'd better not take any chances. Let's go up King Street, off the Quayside altogether and out of view of those busies.'

We started off slowly at first and at the sound of our own footsteps echoing in our ears, we gradually picked up speed until we were running full pelt up the Side and on until we were at St. Nicholas' Cathedral resting by the statue of Queen Victoria.

'I'm sorry for rushing on, I always like the challenge of the hill.'

She looked out of breath and needed time to regain her composure.

'I don't train for the football team like you!'

'More's the pity, I bet you'd be good.'

She didn't reply, but sat quietly.

I looked up at the Queen looking down at us rather disapprovingly. It was distinctly uncomfortable sitting there watching her watching us. I didn't like it, but it gave us time to think.

Angela stood up when she was ready and we made our way to St. Mary's.

There wasn't anybody inside, the priests would be resting after their lunch. We genuflected towards the tabernacle and reverently and systematically searched each row up and down the church until we had completely covered every bench. I wanted us to take a section each, for fear of being too long, but Angela wanted us to do it together. So we did. A threepenny bit and five pennies was our haul.

'Better than nothing and I'm sure the good Lord won't mind. We'll pay it back one day.'

'We haven't been to Mass today.'

'I know Angela, it's been worrying me, but I can't see what we can do about it now. The Masses are all finished.'

'Well let's stay here awhile.'

'Yes, alright.'

The missing of Mass continued to prey on my mind.

The stillness of our prayers gave sound to the cathedral as we knelt together, the faint whir of a trolley bus was evident and a train easing to a stop in The Central Station.

We happily stayed, defying someone to find us there, but nobody did and we left as quietly as we came, with dignity, crossing ourselves as we genuflected on leaving our bench. Angela seemed to linger a moment longer before rising to her feet. Our footsteps on the cold patterned tiles echoed and re-echoed as we left them behind. I smiled towards Thomas Plumtree on the way out.

We crossed the road and made straight for The Central Station where we bought some chocolate from the machines. We stopped to stamp our names together on one metal strip. I was ready to set the dial and pull the handle for the first letter.

'Let's make one for each of us.'

I was delighted that she had made the suggestion. I secretly wanted one for myself as well, but was typically uneasy about coming out with it myself, it seemed a bit soft.

We took a precious unhurried moment to take it in turn to wrap each other's around our left wrist.

'Those names look proud and strong together, side by side.'

They did as well and it was vaguely comforting to have that metal strip wrapped around my wrist as a bracelet. The metal was cold, but those celestial names linked by an and gave it hidden softness and warmth.

Outside the station once more and the carefully routed journey up through Pink Lane and back to our secret home behind the walls.

12

There was quite a chill in the street, but the hut wasn't cold, although the fire had died. I busied myself organizing that first and stacking more tarry toots for the night ahead. Angela rushed around organizing food for later on. Before long the temperature was rising smoothly and the pan was boiling away on the top of the stove, ready for that cup of tea.

'And maybe some bread and butter?'

The autumn sunlight, so sharp, so bright minutes earlier, was quickly fading into dusk. The appearance of clouds completely finished the light and with the darkness came the rain. We watched it as it fell and listened to the drops, gently at first, landing on the corrugated roof, gradually gathering momentum until they were bouncing off with shuddering force, but no tell-tale drips could be heard or seen inside. We were water-tight. Angela pointed to a cobweb, rain wet, sparkling on the window, each water droplet a newly formed diamond, the owner nowhere in sight. The grass started to droop under the weight of the storm and puddles rapidly appeared. To the rhythm of the falling rain and the flickering of the flames we danced.

We danced to the shadows on the walls, rising and falling in the heat and glow, a dance of dreams, of innocence, of long ago and before, hypnotic, mesmeric, blending and intertwining each being with its separate spirit moulding into one, flame shadows, people shadows, sound shadows, together blending, combining, mixing elements, flowing into new existence. The blossoming of a glowing, growing serenity, a giant peace as we fell before the fire to lie together with only our breath touching, the rain still making its patterns, the flames continuing the dance for us silently amidst the shadows wondering where we'd gone.

We lay transfixed for ages, or so it seemed, but it couldn't have been for long, because as I stirred myself and stood up, the bubbling pan of water was still well full, little had boiled away. I made the tea. Angela prepared our supper. We sat, ate drank and finished with the chocolate. We were satisfied, even though our food supply was running low, as was the money. I shut my mind off from the reality and enjoyed the moment, leaving the future to be endured.

The cobbles were blasting out their heat, their rich pitch smell thick and relaxing. I packed more on to last us well into the night. We fell asleep holding hands, lying close, sleep coming easily and full. The heaviness of the tarry air, mellow and deep in our head, carried us off.

It couldn't have been very late when I woke. The silence broke my dreams. The rain had stopped, a faint occasional sound as a droplet gathered enough of itself to fall to the ground. The fire was glowing, a seemingly constant, eternal, unchanging, pulsing force. I felt myself rise without trying to do so, Angela's hand firmly held in mine still. She rose with me as one and we were at the window. We looked out, out over the grass, through the shining cobweb and caught in its centre was our friar.

Through the cobweb he came, walking towards us, effortlessly gliding over the darkness in his own light. The soggy grass remained undisturbed in his movement, his arms folded beneath his cloak. His face held a rich smile as he moved towards us. Stretching his hands through time, through the cobweb, through the window he beckoned us to him. He called with his hands, slow in their movements, deliberate, unambiguous, welcoming.

As he gestured we felt moved to meet him, the hut losing its substance and evaporating before us as we shed the centuries and came to him. We were beside him for him to embrace us, his thick black cloak surrounding our shoulders, drawing us to him as we travelled back across the grass. It wasn't wet. It wasn't cold. It wasn't, we were. Beneath the archway, out onto a cobbled way and across the silent, empty, past. Turning through a heavy doorway, he took us beside a trickling spring with a carved image of Mary above it. We paused together to bathe our faces in it and taste its sweetness. Our hands remained in cupped, almost prayerful pose as we turned again to find ourselves entering a dimly lit chapel. It felt cold, marrow bone cold, icy, as he removed his cloak from about our shoulders.

Angela and I stood huddled close together. The

friar turned to us, placing his thin fingers over our eyes. I listened and inside I heard, but no voice spoke,

'What can you see?'

'Angela, what do you see?'

My words were spoken clearly, but unsaid, a deep unvoiced link connecting the three of us. Then we saw.

We saw the chapel in which we now stood, it looked the same, the friar was standing. He had more colour, the lighted candles highlighting his tonsure as he lowered his hood and stood before the altar, his back towards us. His altar server next to him, a blonde-haired girl standing alone close by. The friar looked up to the altar crucifix and spoke.

'In nomine Patris et Filii et Spiritus Sancti. Amen

Introibo ad altare Dei.'

I will go to the altar of God.

The altar boy responded.

'Ad Deum qui laetificat juventutem meam.'

The friar then called on St. Dominic to aid him as the Mass proceeded. Quietly, easily, instantly it followed its appointed course to the sacred consecration, the host raised high above the friar's head, still poised in both hands, forefinger and thumb reverently showing the sacred circle of life. The altar boy softly rang the bell, the blonde girl raised her eyes to the host. As we stood watching, the gentle bell of the Mass gave way to other harsher noises, heavy thundering, clanging, footsteps outside.

Thud, thud, thud.

Metal against wood, noise, noise, louder, sharp, deafening clamour and crash, the splintered wood, the broken door.

The entry, through they charged, a number of them,

soldiers, drunken laughter, swords glinting, eyes blazing, yelling, language unknown, hatred implicit, abuse. On they came without resistance. The altar boy ran to the girl, took her hand and a passage opened as they were allowed to flee. Only the friar remained, host still held high, waiting for the blow to come. The soldiers reached him, the raised host falling on the altar steps. Our friar crumpled on the spot where he'd stood, dark shadows appearing, damp through his white habit. The white host trodden underfoot without thought, stained red beside the writhing priest who stretched his hand out in vain, blood seeped from evil cut wounds. Then to be kicked mercilessly aside by the staggering attackers as they gathered up the chalice, throwing its contents over the body beneath them. The tabernacle, the silver cruets, the candlesticks, the jeweled crucifix, all taken up in heavy arms, clutched firmly, along with their swords. They shouted at the dying figure, then retreating from the scene the clanking fading figures trooped down the aisle, misty, gradually disappearing and gone.

The friar remained, prostrate, arm reaching out towards the fallen host in search of it, unable to reach, remaining lost to him. Silence. Death.

Out of the distance the altar boy returned, the blonde girl by his side. They knelt down by the friar, their hands covering their faces, shaking in their grief. As if caught in a moment of inspiration the girl stopped sobbing and reached out and picked up the fallen host.

Angela gasped as she did and the blonde girl looked across to her, their eyes joining in communion as they nodded to each other. As if prompted, I and the altar boy put our arms around the girls and two couples crossed the threshold, breaking the host in four parts and sharing its intimacy.

The images faded fast and all that remained were the sounds inside.

'Help me, help me finish my last Mass, help me brother and sister of ages.'

The friar's fingers were removed from our eyes, the pictures of the past enmeshed into the present, mingling with the beyond. There he stood before us, a figure of beyond and before, unable to rest, to travel on from his assailants who left him dead and to be dying for ever more.

We understood.

He nodded and knew that we would play our parts. I felt calm, Angela looked warm, a tranquility had returned to the little side chapel again as the friar prepared to say Mass. I helped him robe. Angela stood watching, swaying slightly as I led him to the altar. He walked up the steps, his robes brilliant white, unstained, silken, shimmering, transparent, pure.

'Introibo...'

The friar's final Mass began again, down through the centuries, the wandering soul, walking his journey each night, searching for this night to find the means to his lasting peace. In unrehearsed unison we walked his path, priest, server, congregation, a blessed trinity.

Angela, behind me, a comfort to know I'm not doing this alone. The consecration, the host raised, lowered, the gentle bell,

Listen to that bell, it calls you to me
Look up, the bell says
Look up and see me.

No soldiers now, no bursting of doors, the raising of the chalice, the calling bell, eyes raised, the echoing bell drifting off into the forever.

The friar genuflects, the cracking, breaking of the host. Stillness. The bells again. Soundless, yet full.

Listen to me, they call my name
They're calling you to me
The distant sounds of past
Now mingling with time
Listen and hear.

The communion. His first. Mine. Angela's. The final powerful sweeping blessing.

'Mass is ended. Go in peace'

'Deo Gratias.'

In the calming afterwards, the friar disrobed, called us gently to him wrapping us in his cloak. We moved, behind us returned to its place in history, each pace, returning, what was, to then, giving us now again, caught between the darkness of the past and our own present isolation, with the warming comfort of our friar, the only link.

The continuing walk, no wet, no sound, no sky, no night, no day, nothing, a bodiless, drifting movement.

The light returned in our garden as we saw the glowing fire through the hut window. We were inside looking out. There he went for the last time, a smile, a turn, a drift across, over and beyond, disappearing into the night, the past catching up with eternity, his eternity with black night remaining.

Angela was lying beside me, our hands tight in each other's grip, close, looking, sharing.

'We've been to Mass today, we don't need to worry about confession.'

The moon appeared out of nowhere, large and full through the window, the clouds gone, the stars took on a cold glow.

Angela remained looking at me, unmoving, staring into me. I tried to hear what she was saying, but the distance of time was between us. The gas jets were beginning to burst through the melting, sizzling tar, filling the hut with its only sound. We closed our eyes again to sleep, together, as one.

13

It was the moaning that stirred me first from a deep dreamless sleep, then the writhing and piercing scream had me sharply awake.

'My head! My head, it's burning. I can't see the fire. My eyes! I can't see anything. I can't see you, what's happening to me?'

The fire was still glowing warm and the moon made the room bright.

'Help me, please help me.'

She reached out for me. I took both her hands and looked at her lying there frightened, clutching hold of me, not wanting me to leave her. I knew I'd have to leave her, she needed a help that I couldn't give her.

'It's all right love, don't worry, I'll go and phone for help. Be still now, be calm, listen to the night and paint the pictures in your head. Breathe easily, think about tonight.'

'Please don't leave me, I'm frightened, I don't want you to be away from me for a second, please.'

'I must, I must, for your sake. You need help, I must

go, I won't be long, I won't. I promise.'

Breaking free of her hold was the hardest thing I'd ever done in my life. I wanted to stay and comfort her and be there. I was frightened about what I might find on my return.

I stroked her forehead and gently smoothed back her long blonde hair over her head and behind.

'What a lovely forehead you have, I've never seen it before, you've always had it covered. It's so smooth so pale.'

After a while she calmed and gradually I was able to convince her that what I had suggested was right and the only way.

I bent over her and whispered in her ear,

'I'll be as quick as I can.'

She turned her eyes, registering nothing, but she smiled a slow, soft movement lingering long, fighting a deep-felt pain as it stayed.

I could feel the tears filling my eyes as I ran from the hut, across the mud-puddled grass, through our door and out, down to the phone box in Charlotte Square.

'Can I have an ambulance please, it's very urgent.'

They needed little convincing, my voice conveyed it all.

I rushed back to the hut. I was afraid. There she lay on our red blanket, our magic carpet, breathing hard. Then I couldn't hear her breathe. I bent down and felt her heart beat. It was thumping away. The bells. I heard the bells break the night and rushed out to show myself at the gate.

The ambulancemen laid her so carefully on the stretcher and covered her up to her chin. They were the same men who'd carried her across the playground such a little time before. It seemed a lifetime ago.

'You'd better come with us as well.'

I folded our red blanket, warm to each movement and carried it with me, following the stretcher out through the hut door. I stopped to close the hut door for the last time.

I sat in the back of the ambulance next to Angela, her face looked pale, her eyes were closed. I wanted to cry, but determined not to, until the pressure became too great and I buried my head in our blanket and let the anguish flow. I could smell her smell in the blanket, mixing with the sharpness of my tears, the softness of her body filled my head as I cried.

The flurry of activity overwhelmed me as we reached the General. Angela was rushed away while I stood looking after her, clutching a cold, wet, red blanket. The clock struck four and I felt myself slipping down and away from it all.

A flow of words.

'A clot on the brain…'

'The air raid shelter fall…'

'It could have happened any time…'

'Or not at all, no evidence before…'

It had crept up on her in the night, breaking our peace.

'There was little chance... She's slipping away.'

Her life slipping away without her having any further knowledge of herself. Lying fresh and sweet with her gentle smile, radiant on her whole face, the pain gone from behind the smile. Perfect.

Now you're part of the reality of afterwards, whose

hand touched us so little time before. Please let me come with you. Hear me inside, listen.

'Don't go!'

'There's no stopping.'

'Stay! Stay! Please!'

'It's not up to me anymore, I've no say now, our time's past. Goodbye. Remember the peace we had. Our richness. Goodbye, my love, don't be sad. We had a lifetime together. I see our friar over there in the distance. He's calling me, cloak open, arms outstretched, smiling eyes. Welcoming. The lights are bright now. I see him clearly, I'm moving on, up, on, drifting onwards, lifting away. Farewell, don't be lonely, build your strength from us. Keep a corner inside for us to dwell. Go forward, be strong, take care. Goodbye.'

The piercing light bursting in my head, bursting, exploding into blistering eternal darkness, then cold. Then nothing. Then me.

The mumbling sounds of heavily controlled whispering, hoping to be heard and the squeaking of a trolley needing oil brought me back to now. My eyes open, a hospital bed. My mam and dad sitting together, looking at me.

'Hello son', they said together.

I looked at them both. I reached over my hands towards them and felt a comfort from them that I'd never experienced before, smiled and closed my eyes.

*

'Dad! Dad! Are you alright?'

'I'm fine son, just fine.'

I took a handkerchief out of my pocket, dabbed my eyes and blew my nose.

'I was worried about you, you seemed to be miles away, standing there, staring.

'Aye son, you're right. I was. Miles away and far away besides.'

We crossed the road and became part of the bustle that was making for the ground.

'Do you know something, I just remembered one time we lost to Everton two-one when I was a lad, a long time ago.'

'Were you there Dad?'

'No son I wasn't. I didn't manage to make that game, in fact for once I chose not to go.'

'That's not like you Dad.'

'You're right it wasn't like me, but I remember that day very well.'

I tenderly put my arm around his shoulder.

'I'll tell you all about it one of these days.'

We came close to each other and together we hurried along.

ABOUT THE AUTHOR

Michael Louis Hedley was born within sight of the Tyne Bridge. He attended a Dominican Preparatory School and progressed to Ushaw College to train for the priesthood. His career moved on to teaching, travelling to Hong Kong and Germany and to becoming a head teacher in Cleveland. Michael went on to run a retreat centre with his wife in County Durham and to practice as a professional homeopath.

Michael is author of many short stories, articles for educational and spiritual journals, and a published poet. His most recent work is a novel based on the life of John Wycliffe.

Married with five children and a passionate follower of Newcastle United, Michael continues to write and lives in Newcastle and France with frequent sojourns to Iona.

www.michaellhedley.com

29875513R00071

Printed in Great
Britain
by Amazon